"Take your gu[...]
on the ground."

Fargo eyed the circle of rifles aimed at him, Jody, and the other three prisoners. He cursed under his breath as he lifted his Colt from its holster, and let it drop to the ground.

"We're not carrying anything, and we're not Stenson's people," Fargo said.

"Doesn't much matter. We'll show you what happens to anyone on Tillman land without permission," the man said. He pointed to one of the prisoners. "Start with him," he ordered. The guards seized the prisoner, lifting him from the ground, and threw him into the flume.

"No! Jesus, no!" the man screamed as he hit the bed of water inside the chute. His fingers desperately tried to claw at the wet sides of the V-shaped flume, only to slip off helplessly.

A hurtling log came into view, rushing down the flume with the speed of a runaway locomotive. The terrible sound drowned out the man's scream and, in a split second, the huge log smashed into him. Fargo saw the air turn red as sprays of scarlet rose upward. He started to advance toward the chute, then saw the rifles swing around at him.

"You're next, Fargo," one of the men said. . . .

THE TRAILSMAN

#209

TIMBER TERROR

by

Jon Sharpe

A SIGNET BOOK

Signet
Published by the Penguin Group
Penguin Putnam Inc., 375 Hudson Street,
New York, New York 10014, U.S.A.
Penguin Books Ltd, 27 Wrights Lane,
London W8 5TZ, England
Penguin Books Australia Ltd,
Ringwood, Victoria, Australia
Penguin Books Canada Ltd, 10 Alcorn Avenue,
Toronto, Ontario, Canada M4V 3B2
Penguin Books (N.Z.) Ltd, 182–190 Wairau Road,
Auckland 10, New Zealand

Penguin Books Ltd, Registered Offices:
Harmondsworth, Middlesex, England

Published by Signet, an imprint of Dutton NAL, a member of Penguin
Putnam, Inc.

First Printing, April, 1999
10 9 8 7 6 5 4 3 2 1

The first chapter of this book originally appeared in *Arizona Renegades*,
the two hundred eighth volume in this series.

 REGISTERED TRADEMARK—MARCA REGISTRADA

Printed in the United States of America

The Trailsman

Beginnings . . . they bend the tree and they mark the man. Skye Fargo was born when he was eighteen. Terror was his midwife, vengeance his first cry. Killing spawned Skye Fargo, ruthless, cold-blooded murder. Out of the acrid smoke of gunpowder still hanging in the air, he rose, cried out a promise never forgotten.

The Trailsman they began to call him all across the West: searcher, scout, hunter, the man who could see where others only looked, his skills for hire but not his soul, the man who lived each day to the fullest, yet trailed each tomorrow. Skye Fargo, the Trailsman, and the seeker who could take the wildness of a land and the wanting of a woman and make them his own.

Montana, 1860, the logging country
just north of the Sapphire Mountains,
where trees were not the only thing
cut down and the two-legged timberwolves
were worse than the four-legged kind . . .

1

"Coming events cast their shadows before them."

The big man with the lake blue eyes uttered the phrase as he guided the magnificent Ovaro between two towering Ponderosa pines, his voice colored with wry amusement. Written by a man named Joseph Campbell, the phrase had stayed with Skye Fargo ever since he'd first read it. It had proven itself to be true all too often, but always when hindsight had given the proverbial shadows form and meaning. Everyone knew that hindsight was always too late to be of practical help, and shadows, Fargo reflected, were hard to interpret. Even for a trailsman.

His clear azure eyes narrowed as they swept the rugged terrain. Certainly the high-mountain country of northern Montana held plenty of shadows of its own. Named "Land of the Mountains" by the Spanish conquistadors, it was a land that offered both pleasure and hardship, beauty and danger, in equal measure. As he rode from the north, the Sapphire Mountains in front of him and the Bitterroot Range rising in the distance on his right, he wondered if his time with Abbey had been one of those events that cast shadows. It had to be a good shadow she cast, benign and filled with pleasurable memories. Her eager passion, unrestricted ecstasy, and ample breasts could cast nothing else. He had made the long detour into the north Montana high country, hoping she still ran the small sheep ranch with her brother. When he discovered that she did, together they turned the clock back to old pleasures with new urgency.

He'd spent almost a week with Abbey and he smiled as he rode, a parade of intimacies and memories surrounding him. He'd been surprised at how little things he'd thought were forgotten leaped up at once as though they'd simply been waiting for a time to wake. Abbey's nipples were two of those memories, always so very small on her large breasts, as though they really ought to belong to a very small young girl. But her tiny protuberances were fountains of sensitivity, stiffening at once, reaching upward to give and be given. It had always been that way with Abbey and time hadn't changed that at all. The week that followed had been all he could have hoped for, and she acknowledged the feeling was mutual when the week drew to an end.

"You have to go," she had said as she lay exhausted beside him, her slightly chunky body quivering with spent passion. "I'm not getting any of my work done. All my chores are piling up. Go, or stay with me for always," she added. "And I know you won't do that."

He didn't answer, but they both knew she was right. She'd clung to him before he left after breakfast, leaving only shared regret. Shadows, he grunted. If they were being cast by coming events they could only be good ones. Shaking off idle thoughts, he steered the Ovaro down a deer trail as he scanned the land. He always felt small riding this land. The tremendous Douglas firs, Engelmann spruce, ponderosa pines, the giant sequoias, and the red cedar were giants that could make anything and anyone feel small. The evidence that this was logging country was almost everywhere he looked; the stumps of fallen trees, the broken pieces of a bucking saw, the long hafts of a splintered falling ax, and the ubiquitous, hooked oil cans were all left lying on the forest floor.

But mostly, the land was imprinted by the thousands of logs that floated down every river, tributary, lake, and waterway. Still more logs could be seen stored in big ponds behind splash dams, built for this exect purpose, waiting for the moment when the spill gate of the dam would be pulled away and the cascade of logs would be sent hurtling down to the river or lake beyond. Riding through logging country always gave him a mixed feeling, Fargo acknowledged to himself. There was a violation here, the power and beauty of nature destroyed by man's uncaring greed. Someday a better way of using the timber would be found in place of the unchecked logging practiced now, he told himself. There had to be, if the treasure of the great forests were to be renewed for others. But now there was a headlong selfishness, a dark spirit of destruction that affected the destroyers as well as the destroyed. These loggers were a breed unto themselves, he knew, personally brave and foolhardy, the lumber-jacks simply crude and unthinking, their bosses adding avarice and contempt to their legacy.

Fargo turned the Ovaro along the edge of a narrow river, into the open sun that made the horse's jet-black fore-and-hindquarters glisten, and its pure white midsection gleam. Fallen logs all but filled the narrow river, moving faster than they seemed to move from a distance, with no room between them as one pushed against the other. Suddenly his eyes spotted a figure almost in the center of the flotilla of logs. The man lay facedown, his legs hanging into the water, caught between the one log he clung to and the other that held him pinned against it. Fargo sent the pinto into a canter, down a steep bank that deposited him at the water's edge. He peered across the carpet of logs that moved swiftly down the river. They were gathering speed as they moved into the center of the river, jostling each other with increasing force.

Fargo pulled the pinto to a halt, swung from the saddle, and leaped onto the nearest log that drifted past him. Landing on both feet simultaneously, he felt the logs instantly move under his weight. The movement was slight, but it was enough to send some of the logs immediately climbing over others. Though he didn't wear the cleated, caulked boots that loggers wore, he began to make his way across the logs, leaping lightly from one to the other. But the logs moved unexpectedly, some sinking down, others shifting away, and he soon found each step a tricky little dance with the creak and scrape of logs his only rhythm. Fargo's eyes went to the still figure as he became more convinced the man would be crushed as soon as the logs that held him began to gather speed when they reached midriver.

Leaping forward more recklessly, Fargo neared the figure, finally halting on the log that trapped the man's legs. Dropping down, Fargo used both feet and all the strength of his powerful leg muscles to push against the adjacent log. It moved, even with the pressure of all the other logs against it, opening up enough room for him to reach out and swing the man's legs out of the water and onto the log on which he lay. Straightening up, Fargo stepped onto the log and knelt down on one knee to turn the man onto his back. A frown dug into Fargo's brow as the figure wouldn't turn. Leaning closer, he was about to try again when he saw the two big tenpenny nails that had been driven into the log. Ropes ran from the nails around the man's wrists.

His frown digging deeper, Fargo stared at the figure. The man hadn't fallen and been trapped by the crush of adjoining logs. He'd been purposefully nailed to the log and sent out into the river with the mass of other logs, to be crushed to death when the logs gathered speed and climbed over each other. But death hadn't waited to claim him, perhaps mercifully so, Fargo noted. The logs that had trapped his legs had also taken his life from him, probably by sheer loss of blood. Sitting back on his haunches, Fargo's eyes riveted on the lifeless figure, as thoughts whirled inside him. If the man were found crushed by other logs, the wrist ropes would have been torn away. Had it been a clever way to hide a killing? Or had he been put there on purpose, to be an example for others?

Didn't much matter, he told himself. Either way, it was a cold-blooded killing. The reasons wouldn't change that. They'd only put a face on it, nothing more. He'd let others struggle with that, in their own way, in their own time. He was but passing by. A bitter taste stayed in his mouth as he rose to his feet and began to hop his way across the treacherous, shifting floor of logs. Suddenly a huge redwood rose up, driving itself forward over another log and straight at him with thunderous speed. He spun, half leaped, and landed on a nearby log, then jumped onto another, continuing to find his way over the logs. Finally, with a long jump, his feet hit the soft earth of the shoreline.

Turning, he watched the logs gathering speed as he slowly walked back to where the Ovaro waited. Questions still clung to him as he pulled himself onto his horse and rode up the embankment, away from the waterway. He rode south again, refusing to dwell on what he'd seen, though the other logs that drifted by as he rode refused to let him forget. He was passing through, he reminded himself again, and he'd let it stay that way.

Moving through the thick forests of red cedar and lodgepole pine, he heard the distant sounds of logging operations; the crash of the huge trees that reverberated for miles, the sounds of big, double-handled bucksaws, and the sharp crack of broadaxes. The noise faded away as he rode deeper into untouched, virgin timberland, and as the day began to slide into dusk, he slowed to a halt.

He listened, his head inclined to one side, his eyes scanning the forest from beneath the frown that had again perched on his forehead. He sat very still, his wild-creature hearing focusing on sounds that had intruded on him since he'd entered the virgin forest. This time it was the whir of wings taking flight, and an entire charm of goldfinches with their black foreheads and black wings soon filled the sky. Before that, it had been a herd of black-tailed deer, all fleeing the forest at once, startled and fearful of an alien presence. There had also been the tremendous racket of a murder of crows, the kind only set off when they were unexpectedly disturbed. Crows, being what they are, didn't just fly away as most birds would. They stayed, swooped in huge groups, angrily cawed and protested, and aggressively showed their displeasure. When they finally calmed down, Fargo could hear the unmistakable rustling sound of a grouse taking wing almost straight up into the sky.

It had all been a good distance behind him yet it had persisted, one sound after the other, each a message to those who could understand. He had ridden casually, making no effort to cover his tracks, but he was becoming convinced that either someone was following, searching out trailmarks, or happened to be riding along the same paths as he. Fargo grunted at the last thought. He never dismissed coincidence. He just didn't put much store in it. As night supplanted dusk, he swung from the Ovaro, and led the horse into a dense thicket of hackberry with plenty of wild geranium to soften the land and welcome a bedroll. He ate cold beef jerky, certain that darkness

7

had put a stop to anyone tracking him. Then he lay down and listened to the night sounds—the clatter of scarab beetles, the buzz of insects, the soft swoosh of bats, the chatter of kit foxes—until finally he slept.

When morning came he found a stream, washed, and rode on until the trees thinned out enough to leave patches of open land. He stopped, dismounted, and used his boots to scrape marks on the ground, pressing a circle in the grass. He used his canteen to damp down the grass inside the circle. Once finished, he then added a few more meaningless marks and smiled. Even he wouldn't know what to make of them. Taking the Ovaro behind a cluster of cottonwoods, he sat down against the furrowed, pale bark and waited. The sun had reached the noon sky when he heard the horse approaching in clustered, hesitant steps, the rider pausing often to search the ground.

Fargo was on his feet behind the tree trunk when the horse pushed into sight. It was a dark brown gelding, the rider on it no more than eighteen years old, Fargo guessed, as he took in the young man's smooth cheeks and full, unruly black hair. The youth halted, dismounted, then knelt down beside the markings on the ground. Fargo watched the scowl of consternation gather on his forehead as he studied the markings. "Real confusing, isn't it, junior?" Fargo said, stepping from behind the tree. "What do you make of it?" Startled, the young man straightened up and spun around, one hand moving toward the gun at his hip. "I wouldn't do that, junior,"

Fargo said quietly. The youth's hand dropped to his side as his eyes went to the marks on the ground.

"You make these?" he asked.

Fargo smiled as he nodded. "Figured they'd give you something to wonder about," he said.

"They did. I'd have spent hours trying to figure them out. Why didn't you go on?" the youth asked.

"Curiosity," Fargo said. "You've been following me."

"Been following tracks, hoping," the young man said.

"Hoping for what?" Fargo queried.

"That you'd be Skye Fargo," the youth said.

"What made you figure I might be?" Fargo asked.

"Heard you were staying at Abbey Carson's. I stopped there. She told me you'd gone on due south. I followed. Yours were the only single rider tracks I came onto."

"If I were Skye Fargo, what then?"

"There's somebody wants to see you. I was sent to find you," the young man said.

"Who, why, and what for?" Fargo asked.

The youth started to answer, but he had only opened his lips when the shot rang out, the heavy crack of a rifle. Fargo saw the young man's unruly black hair bounce in all directions as the bullet smashed into him. Clutching his side with a groan, he fell as another shot rang out, followed by more. Fargo hit the ground as he saw the riders racing into sight. Six, he counted automatically. They were still concentrating their fire on the young man stretched out on the ground but Fargo rolled, flinging himself into the trees as bullets began to kick up dirt inches from him. The brush closing over him, Fargo yanked the Colt from its holster as he saw the attackers start to come after him. Two led the charge as Fargo aimed, then fired. The two men dropped from their horses as if they'd both been pulled off by an invisible rope. The other four immediately swerved into tree cover, and Fargo took the moment to retreat behind the trunk of a big cottonwood.

He heard the young man on the ground moan and the four riders dismount, as they started to come after him on foot, staying in the trees. They were overeager, hired guns, he saw, and they stayed too close together as they moved toward him. He raised the Colt, steadied the gun against the tree trunk, and let one of the figures move into sight, another at his heels. Both were in a half crouch but moving too quickly, their overeager amateurism obvious. The Colt barked twice, the second shot aimed only a half inch away from the first and both figures went down at once. Fargo waited, and heard the other two halt, then crouch. They were suddenly uncertain, fear gripping them in its paralyzing hold. His ears picked up the sound of their feet sliding backward, suddenly turning to run. Fargo shifted his position to the other side of the tree trunk, his gaze fixed on the spot where they had first ridden into the trees.

It was only a few seconds before the two horses burst from the trees, racing over the open ground to reach the thick tree cover from which they'd first appeared. Fargo had time for only one shot, and choosing the rider on the right, he fired. The man fell forward, hitting the saddle horn, and the motion of the galloping horse did the rest, tossing him into the air to hit the ground with a resounding thud. The last rider raced on, vanishing into the trees as Fargo listened to the sound of his horse diminish as it fled. Holstering the Colt, Fargo ran forward to the young man, knelt down beside the red-stained figure, and saw he was still breathing. Grimacing, Fargo took in the extent of the wounds that soaked the youth's clothes with blood. At least four bullets had hit him, Fargo saw. The youth managed to lift his head a few inches from the ground. "Easy, take it easy," Fargo murmured.

"Tillman . . . Darlene Tillman . . . waiting for you," the young man managed to gasp. "Important . . . go see her." The effort took the last of his strength, his words ending with a final gasp. Fargo leaned back as he softly cursed. He rose after a moment, and walked to where the other figures littered the ground. He examined each one and found nothing to help him. But *someone* had sent them to find the young man and stop him before he could deliver his message. They had almost succeeded, Fargo grunted angrily. Almost.

His eyes went to the young, slender figure. The youth had given his life in his assignment. Somebody better have a good explanation, Fargo thought bitterly as he went to the youth's horse. He drew a blanket from the saddlebag and wrapped it around the silent, bloodstained figure.

He lifted the youth up, laid him across his own saddle, then walked to the Ovaro. Holding the reins of the brown gelding in one hand, Fargo slowly started to ride on south. He'd no way of knowing that south was the way to go, and he hoped he'd find somebody that might help. As he rode, he tried to piece together the few bits and pieces of information he had. The young man had visited Abbey, looking for him. That meant he had to have first visited Ed Stanford up near Ninepipe. Ed was the only one who knew he was going to visit Abbey, Fargo recalled. They'd spent a few days talking after he'd broken the trail from Idaho Territory for Ed. But Ed had probably told enough others he'd hired the famous Skye Fargo to break a trail for him.

So the boy finding out that he had visited Abbey was explainable. The youth had followed him south, picked up his trail, and met his death because of it. A Darlene Tillman had hired him, he'd muttered with his last breath. Not much to go on but it would be enough. Fargo had found trails with slimmer leads. He felt a stale bitterness inside him, first at what he'd witnessed, and then at being plunged into something he knew absolutely nothing about. The young man had been a total stranger, yet now he was suddenly no stranger at all. He was someone with whom Fargo had become involved. That imposition angered him, Fargo realized. He had certainly no responsibility for the youth's death, yet still, a kind of oblique responsibility had been thrust upon him.

Damn, Fargo swore as he found himself thinking about coming events that cast their shadows before them. If he had not stayed the glorious week with Abbey, he would have been long gone from this north Montana country. If he hadn't told Ed Stanford he was going to visit Abbey, the man wouldn't have been able to tell the youth. There'd have been no one to trail him, to purse him with still undelivered messages. Coming events did cast their shadows, he grunted, but you could only understand them long after they'd been cast.

What shadows was he riding into now, Fargo wondered as he moved past another lake half filled with logs, a big splash dam holding back hundred of other logs. Perhaps he'd be wise to let the brown gelding behind him find its own way, he pondered. But he wouldn't, he knew. The young man wrapped in the blanket behind him deserted to have his message delivered. Everybody deserved some kind of obituary.

2

A road that was little more than an elk trail or logger's path came into sight and Fargo followed it through a long stand of box elder. He passed two heavy, four-wheel log trucks built to be drawn by horses or oxen, their forty-inch-high wheels carrying extra-wide rims. A few miles further, the town rose up unexpectedly, as though it had just been dropped there—no cleared land around it, no farms spreading out on the perimeter, as with most towns. A wooden sign hammered into the ground greeted him as he drew closer to the town, the single word HIGHTOP carved into it. The road led through the center of the town, and was the town's only real street.

Fargo rode between ramshackle buildings, saw a barber shop with its pole in need of restriping, a few sheds, a small general store, a blacksmith's shop, and a narrow, two-story house with a bed-and-board sign over the door. It was not much of a town, he grunted to himself, slowing before the saloon, which was the largest structure in the town. He noted a half-dozen young women visible in the windows of the tavern's second floor. Owensboro mountain wagons lined the street, along with a handful of buckboards and one-horse spring wagons. Two men came out from the saloon as he passed, and as Fargo pulled to a halt, he saw their eyes cut to the blanket-wrapped figure lying across the gelding. But they said nothing. It was the kind of town where curiosity didn't bring questions, where the unusual was usual.

"Howdy," Fargo said with friendly casualness. "Looking for somebody. Name's Darlene Tillman."

"That'd be Tillman Logging," one of the men grunted, spitting out the juice of a wad of chewing tobacco from his mouth.

"Where might that be?" Fargo asked.

"You'll be going west when you leave town. Keep on the road till you reach Three-Rock Pyramid. Take a left turn and keep going into the Cabinet Mountains, past Flathead Lake. That's Tillman Logging country. The Tillman place is deep into it."

"Much obliged," Fargo said. He saw the man start to say more, but then he pulled his mouth closed. "Something more you want to say?" Fargo questioned.

The man's eyes darted again to the figure across the gelding's saddle. "You could wind up like him in that country," he said pointedly.

"Why?" Fargo frowned.

"Lots of reasons," the second man suddenly said.

"The Tillmans don't like visitors?" Fargo prodded.

"They're not the only ones," the first man said, chewing thoughtfully. Fargo could see that he would get no more answers.

"I'll remember that," Fargo said nodding his

head, then he moved on as the two men walked toward a loaded wagon. The town ended a few dozen yards further down and Fargo followed the road beyond it, as the tree cover thickened and the path narrowed. Finally, he came to the three flat stones that were piled to form a crude pyramid, and Fargo circled them, continuing down the road to his left. He'd only gone on another hundred yards when he suddenly found himself in country that towered on both sides of him. He was surrounded by huge growths of blue spruce, lodgepole pine, and red cedar. The heavily timbered land seemed to go on without end; thick foliage on both sides of the road, seemingly impenetrable forests with huge, thick trees crowding one another. But Fargo saw wagon marks on the road, the wide-rimmed treads of logging rigs, and he continued to follow the road, knowing it would lead somewhere. When the sun drifted into the afternoon, the forests grew dark, becoming an eerie world filled with strange, shadowy shapes. Fargo rode with every sense alert, the tobacco-chewing man's warning returning to haunt him. He had gone another few miles when he became aware of flitting forms that suddenly appeared in the forest at his left.

At first he thought it was simply branches moving in the breeze, but he realized there was no wind. He peered harder, wondering if his imagination was playing tricks on him, the semidusk and the intertwined branches creating their own shifting images. But again he caught a quick, darting form amid the trees, then another, and then still more. His hand went to the butt of the Colt at his side, remaining there as he kept his slow, steady pace. Wrapping the reins of the gelding around his saddle horn, he let the Ovaro follow the road as the darting shapes continued to flee through the forest. They stayed up with him, but kept to the trees as Fargo gave no sign he had seen them.

The Flathead and the Kootenai shared this land, he knew. While neither was exactly welcoming, they were not the deadly marauders of the fierce Plains tribes. But the Nez Percé also drifted down into upper Montana, Fargo reminded himself, and they were an aggressive, warlike lot to rival any band of Sioux or Cheyenne. He rode cautiously, with his mouth a thin, grim line, but the forest shapes made no move to leave their thick cover. Fargo had just rounded a small curve when he abruptly pulled to a halt. A row of figures stretched across the narrow road in front of him. Not Kootenai, Flathead, or Nez Percé, he saw—not tribes at all but a double row of children, ranging from nine to fifteen years in age, Fargo guessed. He saw boys and girls, most of the boys shirtless, the girls wearing shapeless, one-piece garments. They stared back at him, their young faces serious, unsmiling, an air of threatening hostility in their expressions.

Each held some sort of weapon, mostly slingshots of the kind that could kill a small varmint or crack a man's skull. Fargo heard a rustle of leaves, and glanced up to see more of them in the trees, perched on low branches. A boy Fargo guessed to be fourteen, his blond hair cut short, with a rock in his slingshot, stepped forward. Two younger boys followed him, each with their own loaded slingshots.

Fargo's eyes went to the trees again. Although they were simplistic, he knew the power and accuracy of a slingshot. If they all fired at once, there'd be no escaping the hail of rocks. A few of the boys also carried knives, he noted. The blond boy took another step forward. "Got any money?" he asked.

"Some," Fargo said.

"We'll take it," the boy said. "Your gun and horse, too."

"You playing highwaymen?" Fargo asked mildly.

"Nobody's playing," the boy said with a show of resentment.

"Nobody," a boy next to him echoed in emphasis. Fargo grunted softly in disbelief. They were just kids, children robbed of their innocence, of their childhood. And by an adult, most likely, perhaps more than one. But that didn't make them less dangerous. They'd act out of misplaced bravado and the fears that swirled around inside them. He'd have to play it out, Fargo knew. He had no other options. He was counting on the hope that their childhood had not been easily erased.

"You really been getting away with this?" he asked.

"Everybody we stop," the boy said, proudly.

"Not this time," Fargo said and drew the Colt, aiming it at the boy. He let the barrel move back and forth across the line of young, serious faces. He had the satisfaction of seeing the blond boy's eyes widen, the shock of surprise come into his blue orbs.

"You're bluffing," the boy said, recovering quickly.

"I wouldn't count on that," Fargo said, aiming the Colt back at the boy. "I don't bluff." Fargo waited, seeing the uncertainty in the boy's eyes as he exchanged glances with the others nearest to him. Fargo kept the Colt steady, unmoving, his face impassive.

"You really going to shoot us?" the boy asked, the nervousness in his voice very real.

"Doesn't bother me any," Fargo lied. "You play grown-up, you pay grown-up." He saw worry and confusion in their faces. Childhood clung, he thought in satisfaction. They stared at Fargo's blank face as he pulled the hammer back on the Colt, the click resoundingly loud in the silence. "Move away or get blown away. It's as simple as that."

No one answered, but they all swallowed hard. Fargo kept his own countenance hard, but decided not to push this too far. He didn't want to kill anyone, especially a child, and knew he had to tread carefully. These kids were wrestling with mixed emotions; the realities of childhood and the burden of being thrust into adulthood. That alone was enough to trigger actions that could result in tragedy, so he waited, gave them time to sort out the emotions that ran through them. He was still waiting when he caught the movement in the trees behind them. A figure came forward, pushing its way into sight. The children parted to make an aisle and Fargo saw that the figure was actually a towering man, about six foot eight. He took in the man's long, muscled torso, under a shirt that was hanging open in front, his lean but wiry arms, long legs clothed in ragged jeans; a figure that echoed the lodgepole pines behind it.

The man had reddish hair cut fairly short, an angular face with a long jaw, dark blue eyes, and ruddy, tight skin. In his hands, the man held an old Plains rifle, its long barrel pointed forward. "Hold a minute, mister," the man said. "Don't want shooting. Don't want killing."

"That's nice, seeing as how you could be the first one killed," Fargo said calmly. "Who are you?"

"Jeremiah," the man said.

"You the pied piper for these kids?" Fargo rasped.

"I'm no pied piper. They listen to me, if that's what you're asking," the man said.

"Someone ought to teach them better," Fargo said.

"We do what we have to do," Jeremiah said truculently.

"Teaching kids to play highwayman? Is that what you have to do?" Fargo sneered.

"It's a hard world, 'specially for some," Jeremiah said.

"It's going to get harder, 'specially for you," Fargo said.

"We can settle this without shooting," the man said.

Fargo kept his face immobile. For his own reasons, Jeremiah was not anxious for a showdown. Fargo didn't want to let him think he was of a like mind.

"I'm listening. Make it quick," Fargo said.

"We settle it man to man. They'll watch. I win and you hand over everything. You win and you can ride on," Jeremiah said.

Fargo smiled inwardly. The challenge held a

canny cleverness. Jeremiah didn't want to risk his life, but he didn't want to back down in front of his children's army, either. He wanted to have his cake and eat it too. The challenge was his way to do just that. He seemed plainly confident he could win a one-to-one faceoff. Fargo eyed the towering figure's physique. Jeremiah would be no easy task, yet he had faced bigger ones, Fargo pondered. "Not enough," he spit out, and saw the man's long face frown.

"What do you mean? What's not enough?" Jeremiah said.

"Riding on if I win," Fargo said.

"What do you want?" the man asked.

"I want you to leave these kids alone. No more robbing and threatening folks, no more playing highwayman, no more stealing their childhood from them," Fargo said.

"Others did that before me," Jeremiah protested.

"You're carrying it on. I win, you stop. That's the deal," Fargo said.

"Agreed. We'll put our guns down together," Jeremiah said.

"Not here," Fargo said and surprise flooded Jeremiah's face. "You live somewhere. You all do. We'll settle it there. I want witnesses."

Jeremiah thought for a moment, shrugged, and beckoned Fargo to follow. Fargo sent the Ovaro at a walk after him, as the youngsters fell into line on both sides, following along. He was putting himself further out on a limb if he lost, Fargo realized, but he was also making it impossible for Jeremiah to renege, and that was his main purpose. The man led them deeper through the forest and as Fargo walked behind him, he cast a glance back at his silent burden across the gelding. *Sorry, unexpected detour,* Fargo said silently. *I'm not forgetting.* Jeremiah, walking briskly now, made a right turn, and Fargo saw the denseness of the pine forest thin, as land that had been partly cleared came into sight. Fargo saw a collection of tar-paper, wood, and canvas shacks, some little more than lean-to shelters. A dozen adults stopped cooking, tanning hides, and repairing the shacks, and turned to watch the strange procession move into their midst. Many of the children hurried over to them as more adults appeared, many of the men worn and aged with full, gray beards. Most of the women had enough years on them as well, he saw, clothed in patched dresses, hair stringy and tangled.

But Fargo saw three full-figured younger women, their breasts, hips, and legs prominent in tight, one-piece dresses. One, with long black hair and a sultry mouth, pretty in a little-girl way, hurried to Jeremiah and took his arm as he halted and swept the others with a glance. He told them what had transpired, and what was about to happen. He didn't embellish anything, and Fargo gave him credit for that much. When his finished reciting the conditions Fargo had set, Jeremiah turned, and shrugged his shirt off as Fargo dismounted. "I'll take the guns," a thin man with a straggly beard said, stepping forward. Jeremiah handed him the rifle and Fargo gave him his Colt. The young woman detached herself from Jeremiah and came over to Fargo, her full, firm breasts almost spilling out of the garment she wore. Her sultry eyes scanned his face.

"Smarten up, mister. Just go your way. You don't know what we are, what we do, or why we do it," she said.

"You all family here?" Fargo questioned.

"Only a few of us, if you mean blood family," she said. "Why?"

"Wondered what gives you the right to use these kids," Fargo said.

"That's not your concern," she said, her eyes narrowing.

"It is if I make it so," Fargo said.

Her eyes studied him. "You're real handsome, but real dumb," she said.

"I'll take it from here, Jesse," Jeremiah cut in, starting to move toward Fargo.

"Stand aside, Jesse," Fargo said. "No sense in you getting your dress all full of blood." The young woman retreated to become part of the circle that formed around Fargo and Jeremiah, many of the youngsters settling against the trees to watch. Fargo let Jeremiah's towering form come at him as he rose on the balls of his feet. He was in position, ready to swivel as the man shot out a looping left. Fargo ducked away and felt the blow go past him. His fist barely missed, but Fargo now knew what he wanted to know: the distance Jeremiah's long, lanky arms could travel at full power. He'd also spotted something else. Jeremiah's reach advantage and his quickness were his most potent weapons; but his towering build gave him an awkwardness, his movements were not really fluid or controlled.

Fargo feinted, which drew an immediate response, and ducked under the man's blows. Fargo came in swaying and weaving, meeting another flurry of long-arm punches. He parried them all, but felt the power in Jeremiah's arms as he circled, staying low, weaving as he came in again. Crossing a looping left, following with a long right, Jeremiah stepped in quickly and Fargo felt one of the punches catch him on the top of his temple. It sent Fargo stumbling backward, again aware of the power in those long arms. Ducking, Fargo came in low and Jeremiah loosed another series of blows. But he was punching downward, always a troublesome delivery for even an accomplished boxer, and his blows missed their target. Fargo shot a quick, hard left and right into the pit of Jeremiah's long midsection, two blows that would have doubled up an ordinary man. Jeremiah retreated a half step, emitting two sharp grunts, and with a roar of anger, he drove forward on his long legs, swinging his arms wildly.

Powerful as they were, quick as their delivery, they all missed as Fargo weaved, ducked, and parried, making note of another chink in the man's armor. Jeremiah couldn't shorten up on his punches. If he had been able to do so, his punches would have connected. But his long arms and angular build had its disadvantages as Fargo feinted, ducked, and weaved away again, his opponent charging him with a whirlwind of long, looping punches. Jeremiah continued to come forward throwing punches and Fargo saw the growing frustration in the man's face as his downward, chopping blows only grazed their mark. With a sudden, sideways movement, Jeremiah dodged to his left, then leaned back and swung a roundhouse right. It was an unexpected maneuver delivered with speed and precision, and Fargo felt the blow land alongside his jaw.

An explosion of colored lights went off in Fargo's head and he went down backward. He hit the ground and the shock half revived him, enough to see the towering figure's long right leg kick out. Fargo rolled, and felt the kick land on his side. He continued to roll as Jeremiah's next kick went wild. Leaping to his feet, he crouched low, seemingly dazed as Jeremiah rushed forward, swinging left and right. Fargo avoïded both blows, stayed low, and came in with a short left that caught the man on the side of his long chin. Jeremiah paused and Fargo's right cross landed flush on the point of Jeremiah's jaw. Shuddering, not unlike a tree caught by a sudden gust of wind, Jeremiah wavered in place as Fargo's left came up from a half crouch, the blow delivered with all the strength of his powerful shoulders behind it.

Jeremiah reeled backward, and crashed to the ground as hard as a tree falling. He landed on his back, rolled over, and started to push to his feet. But unfolding his long frame took time. He was still only halfway upright, his arms still low, when Fargo's two quick blows smashed into his face. Jeremiah hit the ground again, sideways this time, and managed to rise to one knee. A stream of scarlet trickled from one side of his mouth as he gathered enough rage to catapult himself forward as though he were a human battering ram. Fargo ducked to the side as the towering figure reached him and hurtled past. Fargo's left lashed out, sinking deep into the man's ribs, and Fargo heard the sharp crack of bone as it split.

Jeremiah gasped out in pain, staggered, and half turned as Fargo's right arched, smashing into his cheekbone. Jeremiah went down as a gash of red opened widely on his face. Hurt and winded, the man still got himself back on his feet as Fargo watched with grudging admiration. He aimed his next blow, a straight left, so that it landed cleanly on the point of Jeremiah's jaw. The tall figure went down, this time to stay. Jeremiah lay still, his chest heaving with deep breaths. Some of the adults rushed forward and knelt down beside him, taking his arms and legs and carrying him off to the side. They laid him softly on the ground and two women produced cloths, washing his cuts as they slowly revived him. Fargo rested on one knee for a moment, and saw the youngsters peering at him wide-eyed, with something that approached admiration in their eyes. "You could take over," the blond boy said.

"No. Didn't come for that. You just stick to the promise he made. That's all I want," Fargo said, pushing to his feet. Jesse's voice cut in and he saw her coming toward him, with less anger in her eyes.

"They'll stick to it. So will Jeremiah," she said as she turned and motioned to him. "Let's talk over here." As he followed her to a small shack and went inside, he saw a single room simply furnished with a cot, chairs, and a small table, with a throw rug on the floor. Drapes covered a clothes closet. She turned and studied his face, gently running a hand over the bruise on his face, a soft, gentle touch. "You all right?" she asked.

"I'll be fine," he said as she sat down on the edge of the cot, motioning for him to sit beside her.

"I'm glad you won," Jesse said. "I shouldn't say that, should I? But you're too handsome to get all beaten up."

"Thanks. That's as good a reason as any not to lose," Fargo smiled, very aware of the throbbing sensuality of her, full, deep breasts all but heaving out of the simple dress. She'd be a terrific distraction, but he just couldn't afford any more. "Where do you fit in here? You Jeremiah's girl?" he asked.

"No," she said firmly.

"But Jeremiah runs the show," Fargo probed.

"No," she said with equal firmness. "He's taken on some things, but we all work together. Jeremiah's really a good person." She paused, studied his face.

"Tell me," he said.

"Everybody here is a son, daughter, or relative of somebody who worked for the big logging outfits. They're here because their fathers, mothers, uncles, husbands, brothers, or guardians were either killed or fired on the job. They were all thrown out, left with nothing, some of the youngest left without even food. In my case it was my father. Most of the kids you see here were rescued by Jeremiah."

"The logging outfits didn't help them at all?" Fargo questioned.

"Not even with buryin' expenses. We came together to fend for ourselves," Jesse said.

"By playing bandits?" he queried.

"Sometimes. Some of us get work in town once in a while. Some of the older people do odd jobs. Sometimes there are crops to be picked, but not often. This isn't farming country. We mostly make what we wear, grow what we eat. But there are some things we have to buy and that costs money."

"So you play highwayman," Fargo said.

"Sometimes," she said with a flare of defiance. "Mostly we stop logging company wagons or payroll riders."

"They let you get away with it?" Fargo wondered aloud.

"Every once in a while they come after us in a posse. But we just disappear into the woods. They end up burning down whatever we built. Then we start up again, in another part of the forest," Jesse said.

"How long do you think you can go on like this?" Fargo asked.

Jesse shrugged. "Some of the older people want to leave, find land someplace we can farm and build a real community. But that'd take time and travel. Good farming land is often in Indian territory. But we keep thinking about doing something. We want to stay together. We've become our own family."

He recognized the truth in her words. They were a family, a family of the abandoned, the disenfranchised. Yet that very burden had given them a strength, a cohesion that could someday help to find their way. Fargo felt both sadness and admiration sweep through him. "The outfits that did your people so poorly, was Tillman Logging one of them?" he asked.

"Tillman Logging's the biggest and the worst of all," Jesse said. "Bill Tillman cares about logs not people. He cuts down people quicker than he cuts down trees."

Fargo took in the anger in her voice. "Thanks for telling me, making me understand you. But that doesn't change our deal. No more holdups. Sooner or later there'll be shooting and you'll get the worst of it."

"We made a deal. We'll stick to it," she said and her hand reached out, covering his. "You could stay with us, help us. We need somebody like you. I'd make you happy if you stayed."

"I'm sure you would but I've my own promises to keep," he said.

She leaned closer and he felt the tips of her full, young breasts brush against his chest, her lust a heady perfume that wrapped itself around him. "Stay. Never asked anyone before to do that," she murmured.

"I'm flattered, and tempted," he said, "but I can't."

"Stop back? Visit? Maybe you'll change your mind," she said.

"I'll try. No promises," he said.

Her lips pressed to his and she leaned forward against him, all warm softness, with nothing under the simple dress but her young, pliant body. She'd be a special pleasure, he was certain, but a special problem, too. She didn't just want a man, though she simmered with wanting. She wanted a tomorrow and that always brought its own problems. "So you'll remember," she murmured, pulling back.

"Definitely," he said and she walked from the shack with him. Jeremiah was standing, the two women and a half-dozen youngsters with him. He walked over a little unsteadily.

"Didn't think anybody could do that to me," he said.

"There's always a first time," Fargo said and realized Jeremiah was really younger than he'd seemed. "Good luck to you," he added.

Jeremiah nodded and Fargo walked to the Ovaro, swung into the saddle, and took the reins of the brown gelding. The small knot of figures watched him, silent and still as he rode from the camp. They had to have learned something, he told himself, and he rode on with quiet hope they'd find their way out of the woods, actually and emotionally. He pulled on the reins in his left hand, and felt the gelding respond. "Time to get on," he muttered.

3

The great forests surrounded him as he rode, at once protective and menacing. The sun had reached late afternoon when the trees finally thinned and in the distance he saw the shining blue of a lake, a mountain river leading down to it. Before the lake came clearly into view, houses rose up, a stone and log main house, first, a collection of bunkhouses spread out behind it. He saw logging equipment scattered about, including timber wagons, their front and rear assemblies joined together with long, rough-hewn "reach" poles cut from forest wood. A dozen men lounged by the bunkhouses and tended to the handful of logs in the lake. Fargo's glance went to the splash dam up in the high water of the river where hundreds and hundreds of logs piled up behind it. He headed for the house, and just before he reached it a woman emerged and came toward him.

She was tall, clothed in a white, tailored shirt that rested on full breasts with a long curve to them. Black riding britches covered slender legs and slim hips. He saw dusty blond hair, worn short, framing a straight nose, high cheekbones, and cleanly etched lips, a handsome, aristocratic face with a hint of arrogance in it. But it was her eyes that held him, the opaque blue of a Siberian husky that seemed to hold both ice and fire in their round depths, eyes that challenged you to see behind them. Two men detached themselves from the others and hurried over as Fargo dismounted, their eyes on the gelding. As they reached the horse, they uncovered the figure under the blanket. "It's Jimmy Donovan," one called out. The woman cast a quick glance at the figure on the gelding, and returned her eyes to Fargo, a tiny furrow creasing her smooth, high brow.

"Six men pumped lead into him while we were talking," Fargo said. "I got most of them. He never gave me his name. His last words were to find Darlene Tillman, said it was important."

"I'm Darlene Tillman," she said with a touch of imperiousness.

"We'll take care of Jimmy," one of the men said and she nodded, her eyes staying on Fargo.

"Please come inside," she finally said and he followed, enjoying the way her slim hips moved, her rear tight under the riding britches. Inside the house, he found a richly appointed living room with velvet drapes, leather sofas, dark wood furniture, and braided rugs on the floor. She turned to face him when they were in the house, her ice-fire blue eyes surveying him with interest and appraisal. "You have to be him . . . Skye Fargo," she said. "Jimmy found you."

"And got himself killed for it," Fargo said.

Darlene Tillman took a decanter and two glasses from a cabinet. "Whiskey?" she asked.

"Wouldn't mind," Fargo said. "Wouldn't mind some answers, either."

"Of course," she said as the curve of her breasts tightened against the white shirt as she leaned forward to hand him the glass of whiskey. "I sent Jimmy Donovan to find you. Of course, I'd no idea this would happen. Obviously, they went to great lengths to stop him from reaching you and you from reaching me."

"Who?" Fargo questioned.

"I can't be sure. Roy Stenson, I'd guess," Darlene said.

"Start from the beginning. Why'd you send for me?" Fargo asked.

"To find my father, Bill Tillman. He disappeared ten days ago. I sent men looking for him but they didn't find a lead. When I heard you were at Ed Stanford's in Ninepipe I had to send for you. That's when I sent Jimmy."

"Unfortunately for Jimmy," Fargo said.

"I can't change that." She shrugged. "But you're here and I still want you to find my father."

"How'd you hear about me?" Fargo asked.

"Talk. Your reputation travels, even all the way up here. I'm sure you've found trails a lot older than ten days," she said.

He nodded. "Your pa disappeared ten days ago. Then you don't know if he's even alive."

"I feel he is," she said. "Of course, he could be hiding somewhere. Or . . ." she left the sentence unfinished.

"Or he could be dead," Fargo said for her. Darlene Tillman's cold-fire eyes bored into him.

"Either way, I have to know. I want you to find him or find what's happened to him. I can't live not knowing. I'll pay you three times your usual rate," she said. Fargo was aware of the conflicting thoughts pounding through him. He felt uncomfortable with the offer, yet he wasn't sure why. Maybe the encounter with the strange, wild family in the forest had something to do with it. Jimmy Donovan's sudden death certainly had rattled Fargo, an event that involved him before he knew he'd be involved in anything. And the strange, circuitous route that had brought him here, foretelling coming events that had already cast their shadows. Darlene Tillman's voice interrupted his thoughts. "You want a better reason to accept," she said.

He smiled as he admired her acuity. "Close enough," he agreed.

"All right, the money's not that important to you. Don't do it for the money. Don't do it for me, either. You don't know me well enough for that. Do it for Jimmy Donovan. He gave his life. He's the innocent one. He deserves justice," she said.

"You've a good way with words." He smiled.

"I've a good way with a lot of things," Darlene Tillman said, her opaque blue eyes suddenly revealing tiny, dancing light in their unfathomable depths. "Find my father and I'll prove it."

"You're making it hard to say no," he answered.

"Exactly," she said, and he considered it for another long moment. She'd made an offer hard to refuse, added intrigue that was impossible to ignore.

"For Jimmy Donovan," he finally said. "Now, fill me in. Who's this Roy Stenson?"

"Stenson Logging, small-time operator. He'd always hankered to move in on Tillman Logging but he's never had the money or the manpower. Maybe he decided that getting rid of my father was the way to go," Darlene said.

"Why now, after all this time?" Fargo queried.

"No idea." She shrugged.

Fargo didn't completely dismiss Roy Stenson, but he took him from the top spot on his suspect list. "Your pa made plenty of enemies beside Stenson," he guessed.

"How do you know that?" Darlene said defensively.

"Men like that usually do," Fargo said, as he thought of how the forest girl had described the ruthlessness of the big logging operators. He heard a sound, and turned to the door to see a young woman that had entered, tall as Darlene but very different in every other way, dark brown hair worn loosely, a soft face, perhaps more sweet than pretty, round cheeks, thin eyebrows, and full lips. She wore a yellow dress, tied at the waist, and Fargo noted her modest breasts and the outline of her full hips and long calves. There was a gentle quietness about her. Only the firm line of her chin that tilted upward showed a hint of determination.

"Didn't know you had company," she said to Darlene.

"This is Skye Fargo. He's the man I sent for to find your Uncle Bill," Darlene said.

The young woman's medium brown eyes

widened instantly and she stepped forward. "Oh, please find him. I'm so worried about him. Bill's always been my favorite uncle. I'm Jody Tillman," she said, her eyes filled with earnest anxiety.

"My cousin," Darlene said and Fargo caught something in her tone, an impatient irritation. "Jody's been visiting from Kansas," Darlene added.

"How long?" Fargo asked politely.

Jody Tillman answered. "Almost a month. I come every year," she said. Fargo studied her again, and decided that she was quietly attractive in her own, understated way. "I'm so worried about Uncle Bill. Can you find him, Fargo?" Jody asked.

"I'll try. That's the best I can do," Fargo said.

"From what Darlene told me that'll be better than anyone else can do," Jody said. She exuded an open sincerity, he saw, a guilelessness that gave her an added youthful attraction.

"I told Jody I'd sent out to reach you," Darlene cut in aloofly. "She was thinking about going out searching herself, a ridiculous idea."

"Probably," Fargo said.

"Probably?" Darlene threw back incredulously.

"My pa used to say that even a blind pig gets an acorn once in a while," Fargo said, as Jody give a quick giggle.

"I'll leave the searching to you, now, Fargo," Jody said. "I'm sure Darlene filled you in on everything."

"I have," Darlene said firmly.

Jody's hands closed around Fargo's arm. "Find Uncle Bill. Please," she said, reaching up and brushing his cheek with her lips. She was hurrying from the room before he could answer. Alone with Darlene, he turned to her.

"She wears her heart on her sleeve," he said and Darlene returned a smile that was polite at best. "How old is she?" Fargo asked.

"Nineteen, though she seems sixteen. She must be kept real sheltered in Kansas," Darlene said.

"She may be a little naive but it's a nice quality, kind of refreshing," Fargo said.

"Kind of childish," Darlene snapped. "I don't understand why men take to it the way they do. They seem to feel so damn protective around her. Even my father goes for her little act."

"Because it isn't an act," Fargo said.

"Whatever, I can't stand her visiting more than once a year," Darlene said. Her resentment of Jody was plain. Perhaps there was some jealousy over Jody's obvious deep affection for Bill Tillman. Fargo could easily imagine Darlene being possessive about anything she wanted for her own. But perhaps it was only a clash of personalities, he reflected.

"Tell me about your pa's leaving. Anyone see which way he went?" Fargo asked Darlene.

"I was still asleep when he left," she said.

"Would he normally leave without saying goodbye?" Fargo queried.

"Sometimes," Darlene said. "Cook found a supply of cans and beef strips gone. But that doesn't mean much."

"Why not?"

"He sometimes went out riding our land for a week. He'd take supplies with him then," she said.

"Wouldn't he tell you when he was going to do that?"

"Sometimes," Darlene said. Fargo nodded but found her answers strangely vague.

"Got any ideas where to start?" he asked.

"Ride west. Most of the Tillman land stretches to the west. That's the way he'd go if he were visiting," Darlene said.

"Maybe I can do better," Fargo said as she lifted an eyebrow. "Passed a town with a saloon in it. Maybe somebody there knows something." He paused, seeing Darlene frown in thought.

"Maybe," she said. There was that vagueness again, he thought, or was she holding something back? It didn't make sense. Holding back wouldn't help him find her father. Fargo finished the whiskey and rose to leave. "When will I hear from you?" Darlene asked, walking to the door with him.

"When I've something to tell you. Or more questions," he said.

Her steely eyes held him. "Find him. I'd like to be really grateful to you," she said.

"I imagine I'd like that, too," he said dryly, stepping outside, where he found dusk sliding over the land. He climbed onto the Ovaro, just as he caught sight of Darlene in a side window. But the yellow dress was now gone, replaced by a dark green blouse and jeans that contoured more of the roundness of her figure. He saw her eyes stay on him as he rode away, feeling concern wafting after him. He wondered idly what had made her change out of the yellow dress. Certainly not to watch him leave, he wondered as the dusk become night, wrapping him in its dark cloak. Picking his way through the brush, he finally arrived at the town, moving down its sole street, past tethered horses and a few buckboards.

He heard the saloon before he reached it, and found a spot at the end of the hitching post to tether the pinto. The diffuse glow of light spilling from the saloon illuminated the row of horses outside. Fargo walked into the large noisy room, took in the battered bar along one side, the sawdust-covered floor, the tables across the room. Most of the customers wore logger's boots, he noted, and he turned to see a woman standing at the foot of the stairway to the second floor. A large figure in a satiny blue dress, bare-shouldered, her heavy breasts straining the fabric, she had a square, jolly face but her eyes were like hard blue crystals. Tight brown curls covered her head and Fargo glanced at the girls that dotted the floor, all deep-breasted with ample bodies that echoed the madam's substantial shape.

Apparently loggers favored robust woman, he decided. The madam's eyes were on him as he approached. "Evening, stranger," she said. "Drink?" He nodded and she gestured to a chair at the table beside her. "I'm Dolly," she announced.

"Bourbon," he said. She snapped her fingers at one of the girls, who returned a moment later with his drink. He sipped it and nodded. "Better than I expected," he said.

"Nothing but the best," the woman said, her eyes taking him in. "Just passing through?"

"Good guess," he said.

"No guess. I know men. You're no logger," the woman said.

"Do clothes and boots make the man?" Fargo tossed back.

"Not just that. Loggers have a look and a certain way about them," the madam said.

"Just like saloon girls," he returned.

The madam allowed a slow smile. "That's one for you," she said, chuckling. "What brings you here, big man? Not a lot of folks come to Hightop."

"Looking for somebody. Thought you might be able to help. I'm sure you hear a lot of things," Fargo said.

"Who are you looking for?" Dolly asked.

"Bill Tillman," Fargo said and saw the madam's face instantly tighten.

"Why?" she questioned sharply.

"Seems he disappeared ten days ago," Fargo said.

"Bill Tillman wouldn't just disappear," the madam said. "If he went somewhere he had a reason."

"He didn't give it to anyone," Fargo said.

"Maybe he didn't want to," the woman replied.

"He disappeared and I want to find him," Fargo stated.

"I'm not helping you or anyone else go after Bill Tillman," the woman said angrily.

"I want to help him. He may be in trouble."

"That's what you say, mister. Talk's cheap," the madam threw back.

"His daughter hired me to find him," Fargo tried.

"Screw her. And you. I don't know anything and

I wouldn't tell you if I did," Dolly snapped. "Maybe you'd best move on, stranger."

"Maybe," Fargo agreed, paid for his drink, and sauntered from the saloon. Outside, he led the Ovaro across the dark street, halting in the deep shadows of a shed. He turned the madam's angry reaction over in his mind. There had been a virulence in it, almost self-protective, that seemed far beyond ordinary friendship. Some sort of loyalty? For what, he wondered as he waited, his eyes on the saloon doors. If he had guessed right, the wait wouldn't be long, he told himself, and it was but a few minutes more when a man came from the saloon. Not a casual, weaving exit, Fargo noted, but a hurried, purposeful stride. It was enough for Fargo and he swung onto the pinto, letting the man disappear on his horse as he headed from town. Following, Fargo stayed back. The night was too dark to pick up hoofprints, so he let his ears guide him.

The horseman turned west and Fargo followed. There was no tentative riding on the man's part. He knew clearly where he was headed. Fargo eyed the quarter moon, and saw that it hung low, past the midnight sky. The horseman slowed as the forest terrain grew more dense and when he passed a hollow, Fargo heard the hoofbeats slow again. Suddenly they came to a halt and Fargo yanked the pinto to a stop at once. His ears twitched, not unlike the Ovaro's, as he listened. No more hoofbeats sounded. The man had dismounted. But Fargo waited, letting fifteen minutes go by before he swung from the Ovaro.

The man had halted for the night, apparently

afraid to lose his way in the dark night forests. He'd sleep the few remaining hours till daylight. Fargo decided to do the same, considered moving a little closer, and then decided against it. He'd wait where he was until morning and pick up the hoofprints when day came. He set out his bedroll, lay down atop it, his ears still alert. But the darkness that stretched ahead of him remained silent and Fargo closed his eyes and let his body relax. He had almost dropped off to sleep when a scream split the night, a woman's voice filled with terror. He sat up and the scream came again, from somewhere behind where he lay. Fargo jumped to his feet when he heard yet another scream, this one different from the first two, much higher in pitch, made not of terror but of fury. It curled through the air, a scream that was also a snarl. It was a sound he knew well, the unmistakable cry of the cougar, not that far away. He ran forward, pulling the Colt from its holster as he did.

Dodging trees in the dim light, he heard the cougar snarl again, closer now, and he raced forward and followed the sound. A small clear half circle came into view, a tall rock at one side, the woman's figure pushed against a tree across from the rock. His glance found the cougar poised atop the rock, its body contracted, ready to jump upon her. Fargo fired on the run, his first shot hitting the edge of the rock, sending up small slivers of stone. The cougar spun and sprang all at the same time, a single moment of fluid beauty. Only he didn't have time to properly appreciate the muscled beast as almost two hundred pounds of furious mountain lion hurtled through the air at him.

He flung himself down and forward, felt the swoosh of air as the big cat all but grazed his head with its giant paw. He half turned, and fired off another shot, but he knew it would only be a warning. The cougar had already disappeared into the trees and Fargo heard it springing through brush in long bounding leaps that carried it away in seconds. He rose, holstered the Colt, and peered across the clearing to the form against the tree. The figure pushed to its feet and he saw the dark green blouse and jeans, the soft-cheeked, pretty face, brown eyes now still round with fright. He was still staring, dumbfounded, when the sound of hoofbeats racing away came to him. "Goddamn," he swore as he whirled, peering after the sound.

The man had to have heard the shots, perhaps the screams. He leaped onto his horse and fled, the safe, smart thing to do. Cursing again, Fargo listened as the sound of the hoofbeats faded away. He stared at Jody Tillman, furious words colliding in his mouth.

"A reason, goddammit. Give me a reason why you're here and it better be a good one," he flung at her.

"I was looking for you," she said, her voice small.

"That's not good enough," he rasped.

"I was following and I lost you. I started walking, trying to find prints and suddenly there was the cougar in front of me," Jody Tillman said.

He glowered down at her. "You know what you just did? You just lost the one lead I had to your uncle."

Her round-cheeked face fell. "Oh, my God. I'm sorry," she offered.

"Sorry doesn't cut it. Why? Why, goddammit?"

"I was very upset. I overheard you and Darlene talking. That's when I heard you were going to visit the saloon in Hightop. But there were things she left out," Jody Tillman said.

He frowned at her, deciding the turmoil in her face was very real. "Where's your horse?" he asked.

"Back there someplace. He ran when he heard the cougar," Jody said.

"Find him," Fargo said and she turned and hurried away. He listened to her calling until she finally returned, leading a brown quarter house. She followed him back to where he had left the Ovaro and he lowered himself onto the bedroll. "Sit down," he said and she came beside him. "Talk. What things did she leave out?" he said sternly.

"She didn't tell you that she and Uncle Bill were having big fights every day before he left. They went on all week, really big shouting matches," Jody said.

"What about?" he questioned.

"I never learned that. Their fights were behind closed doors. I couldn't hear more than the screaming, but they were both very upset after each one."

"You think his disappearing had something to do with their fights," Fargo said.

"I don't know, but I was awake the night he left. I couldn't sleep and I looked out the window, and saw Uncle Bill going into the barn. I went out to the barn, and he was saddling the horse, getting ready to ride out. I asked where he was going at that hour," Jody said.

"You don't hold back, do you?" Fargo said.

"I was concerned for him. Uncle Bill has always been my favorite person," Jody said. "He's kind, thoughtful, considerate. Ever since I began visiting as a little girl he showed me things, did things for me, taught me to ride, taught me about trees, shrubs, rivers. He's a wonderful person."

Fargo nodded, and found it easy to understand Bill Tillman's taking to Jody. She had a disarming directness to her. Perhaps it was part of her naiveté but her openness seemed to reach out, a very beguiling quality. Yet again he thought about the forest family, and about Jesse and her description of Bill Tillman. It was a very different account from the one Jody gave. "Did he tell you where he was going?" Fargo asked her.

"He told me he had his reason for leaving in the middle of the night and I wasn't to tell anyone, including Darlene, that I'd seen him leave. I didn't, of course, but I'm very upset."

"At his leaving."

"At that and everything else," Jody said.

"Such as?" he asked.

"The next day, when Darlene found out Uncle Bill had left in the dead of night, she seemed more angry than concerned and she's been that way ever since," Jody said.

"Maybe you're misinterpreting her reactions," Fargo said. "Some people act in strange ways when they're really troubled."

"Maybe, but it didn't seem right, being so angry.

It still doesn't. I decided I had to tell you. That's why I followed you," Jody said.

When he thought about what she had told him, he found himself unable to stay really angry at her. "You did everything wrong. You lost my lead. But you were trying to do right, I'll give you that," he muttered.

"Thanks," she said.

"There's not a lot of the night left. Let's get some sleep," he said. "You need a blanket?"

"No, I'm warm. I've one in my saddlebag if I do," Jody said and she stretched out atop the bedroll, lying down beside him so that her shoulder touched his. "You may not be glad I came, but I am. I feel better having told you," she said. She half turned, rose up on one elbow, and planted a soft kiss on his cheek. "That's for not letting me become cat food," she said with a shudder.

"Go to sleep," he growled and she lay back against him. She was definitely unafraid to pursue whatever seemed right to her. For all her quiet, open ways, she could obviously summon a quiet determination. Perhaps that was part of her naiveté, too, he reflected. Fargo let weariness take command, and he closed his eyes and slept, stirring only when the dawn sun rose. He sat up, glancing over at Jody. She had opened the buttons of her blouse to stop the garment from pulling on her and he saw the swell of one sweetly modest breast, a soft white mound peeking out from the edge of the blouse. He rose, used his canteen to wash, and watched her wake, sit up, and rub sleep from her eyes. Her brown hair fell across her face, and Fargo saw that her sweet, quiet prettiness was there even when she just awakened. But he knew there was only one thing he could do with her, and he waited until she had freshened up before facing her.

"I'll be taking you back," he said. "Then I'll come back here and try to pick up a trail."

"Back where?" Jody asked.

"The house. You'll be safe there," he said.

"No, absolutely not. Darlene will be furious with me that I left. She'll want to know why I followed you and I'll have to tell her," Jody said.

"It won't make any difference, now," he said.

"She'll make life miserable for me," Jody said.

"You can leave, catch the next stage East."

"From where?"

"Hightop, probably. Or someplace else. You can ask."

"I can't go, not until they send me my ticket back and that won't be for a month," Jody said.

"You can't run around loose in this country," he said.

"I thought I'd go with you," she said.

"No way," he snapped.

"I'll find someplace to stay, a boardinghouse," Jody said.

"Nothing you'd want to stay in around here. I'm taking you back. You may not like it there now, but at least you'll be safe," Fargo said.

"I won't go," Jody said defiantly.

"You'll go, the easy way or the hard way," he said.

She glared at him. "I'll go looking for Uncle Bill on my own," she said.

"You can do whatever you want," he said as her

face softened. "*After* I take you back," he finished and the glower flooded her face again.

"Put away your conscience. I can take care of myself," she said.

"Sure you can. Like with that cougar?" he returned and she made a face at him. "Besides, it's not my conscience. I just don't want you in my way."

She glared for another moment, then gave a shrug. "I guess you're right," she said. "I'd like to change my blouse before we ride. Would you mind turning around?" she asked quietly.

"For you," he said, turned his back to her, and waited.

"I'm sorry, really," he heard her say after a moment.

"You should be," he said, and started to turn around when the piece of wood smashed into the side of his head. The blow didn't land with full force, yet it had enough power to send him falling as red and yellow lights flashed in his head. He felt himself hit the ground, and as he shook away the pain and grogginess, he heard the dim sound of hoofbeats galloping away. Cursing, he pushed to his feet, swaying wildly, and he took a moment to recover before clearing his head and running for the Ovaro. Ignoring the pain in his temple, he vaulted into the saddle and sent the horse into a gallop, his ears straining to pick up the sound of hoofbeats.

He focused on the sound, and heard her turn north, heading for prime logging country. But he also heard her slow as she rode into the dense timber. He kept the Ovaro full out, aware of his horse's ability to move in and out of thick forest terrain. He caught a glimpse of her a few minutes later, and as he took his lariat in hand he saw her cast a quick glance back at him. She was in the middle of thick forest, bent low in the saddle and had to slow her horse again as she guided it through the thick foliage. He drew closer, continuing to ride hard, and sent the lariat spinning through the air. As it fell over her, he yanked the rope tight and slowed the Ovaro at the same moment, sending Jody Tillman flying from the saddle.

She was on the ground shaking her head, when he halted, swinging down from the horse and striding toward her. He reached down and pulled her to her feet. "It seems you can be soft-cheeked, sweet-faced, and a little bitch all at the same time," he growled.

She looked at him contritely. "I'm sorry," she murmured.

"You're making a habit of those two words," he snapped. She shrugged, continuing to look contrite. "But you're going back," he said. His hands moved with quick, deft motions, tying her arms to her sides, then he helped her onto the horse, her flesh warm under his hands.

"You don't have to do this," Jody said. "I won't try anything else."

"Why don't I believe you?" he answered as she rode beside him.

"Because you're just suspicious." Jody sniffed.

"Happens every time I'm tricked and slugged," Fargo muttered. She fell silent as they rode back toward the Tillman place. They were nearing it, the lake glistening in the near distance, when she spoke again.

"You're not being fair. I tell you something's very wrong here. Uncle Bill may be running away from Darlene," she said.

"Why?"

"I don't know." She frowned.

"See me when you have something besides feelings and suspicions," he said. "Meanwhile, I'll look for Bill Tillman my way. That means without your help, honey." They reached the cleared land with the main house and the bunkhouses behind it and he saw at least a dozen fresh saddled horses behind one of the bunkhouses. He rode to a halt in front of the main house as Darlene strode out, her eyes spearing Jody.

"How dare you run away!" Darlene spit at her.

"I didn't run away. I've a right to go look for Uncle Bill," Jody returned.

"I hired Fargo to do that. You mind your own business," Darlene said, her cold blue eyes blazing. "Get in the house," she ordered as Fargo undid the lariat that bound Jody's hands. He saw the quick glance of reproach she flung at him as she stalked into the house and Darlene turned to him. He glanced toward the horses beside the bunkhouse.

"Adding hands?" he inquired.

"Backup," Darlene said. "I'm depending on you but I hired them to search to the south, just in case. I can't expect you to cover the whole territory. I've got more men coming still."

"You're paying," he said.

"Thanks a lot for bringing Jody back. I feel a certain responsibility for her," Darlene said.

"I'm wondering why you didn't mention something she told me about out in the brush," he said. Darlene waited to hear what Fargo was about to say, not giving away anything. "She said you and your pa were having big fights before he left."

Darlene let a slow smile of tolerant amusement cross her face. "That's a perfect example of what you call her naiveté and I call her childishness. Pa and I always argue. We always shout and scream at each other. It's our way. She's just not usually around to hear it." Fargo turned her answer over in his mind. It was entirely plausible, he had to concede. "She's so fond of my pa that she gets carried away by her protectiveness," Darlene said. Fargo nodded, thinking that was easy to believe of Jody. Her open honesty could easily lead to an excess of loyalty and imagination. His thoughts broke off as Darlene linked her arm in his.

"It'll be dusk in less than an hour. You can't search in the dark. Stay the night and start out come morning," Darlene said.

"Why do I think you're not just being hospitable?" He smiled.

"Because you're too perceptive," she said, her arm remaining in his. "I called you in to find my pa. Now, I want more—I want you to find *me*."

"You want to fill that out?" Fargo said.

"I'm worried, afraid, if you like. I may be running Tillman Logging all by myself. That's enough to give anyone pause," she said.

"I suppose it is," he agreed. "But you know something about the operation."

"I'll still need support. I want to feel I'm not all alone. You could give me that, Fargo. I knew that from the first moment I saw you. I can feel things like that, and I'm never wrong." She moved closer, the faint scent of orange water on her skin. "I need you to hold me, understand me, believe in me. Is that such a terrible thing to ask? Is that so wrong?"

"No, not terrible and not wrong," he said. "Just human, I guess."

"Good," she breathed, her lips almost touching his. Her cold-fire eyes flashed at him, a smoldering, smoky blue. "I don't want other eyes on us, raising suspicions, wonderings, loose talk," she said.

"You mean Jody?"

"She, the men, anyone. Take the narrow road east. Go left at the twisted white pine. There's an arbor a ways past it. I'll come after dark," she almost whispered. He nodded and a tiny smile of satisfaction touched her lips as she turned and hurried away toward the bunkhouses. He climbed onto the pinto as dusk began to close in, riding until he found a narrow road. Following it, he soon came to a twisted white pine and kept on until he reached a little arbor which was set back from the road. The dark descended rapidly as he unsaddled the horse and set out his bedroll. The night stayed warm and as he munched on a strip of cold beef jerky and took off his shirt, he felt himself relax.

Darlene was turning out to be more complex and intriguing than he'd expected, all of her echoing her eyes. But then everything that had brought him here had been made of strange and unexpected twists. It was perhaps only fitting that Darlene should be more of the same. He was still thinking about her and the eyes that could so fascinate when he heard the sound of a horse approaching at a walk. He sat up and felt the surprise slide across his face as Darlene came into the arbor on a gray gelding. She halted, her dusty blond hair with an almost silver cast to it in the moonlight. She slid from the horse and stood before him, clothed in jeans and a dark shirt that hung untucked. Her eyes still smoldered as she dropped to her knees on the bedroll. She remained silent, letting her smoky blue orbs speak as she suddenly flicked open the buttons of her blouse and that garment came off, then the jeans, her movements quick and smooth and in moments she was naked before him, a smile edging her lips.

"Very lovely," he breathed, the words not just a polite comment. His eyes lingered on her full breasts, each a long-curved, beautiful pear shape, each tipped with a dark red nipple centered on an areola of matching color. His eyes followed the long waist that dipped down to a flat abdomen and below, the small rise of her belly, a tiny, dark insert in the center. Long legs, a little full yet nicely curved, tapering down to smooth, long calves. His eyes returned to her pelvis where a full, thick dark triangle pushed upward with its own boldness.

Her arms rose, pulled at his belt, and he felt her taking off his trousers. He felt himself already starting to respond to the unvarnished wanting of her. When her lips came to his, her hand reached down. "Oh, oh, jeez," Darlene murmured. "Yes, yes, yes."

Her hand closed around him, pulling, stroking, until his mouth closed on one pear-shaped breast, drawing it in, his tongue tracing around her nipple, already grown firm and wanting. She gave a tiny half cry, her hand caressing his chest as he slowly leaned over her, letting his fingers draw an invisible line down her torso, caressing the soft rise of her belly. He slid down further as his lips sucked on one full breast, then the other. Small moans of pleasure rose from her, little urgings that grew stronger as his hand spread its way to the fine filaments that curled around his fingers from the black triangle. He felt the soft rise of her Venus mound and his hand slid down deeper, coming to the softness of her already parted inner thighs.

The moisture touched his hand at once, dew of desire beckoning wordlessly, and Darlene's lips opened in a gasped cry. Her hips lifted and fell back, then surged upward again, and Fargo felt her hands digging into his shoulders. He slid along her slickened thighs and entered the dark portal as Darlene's scream erupted, her body quivering. Her torso bucked upward, entreating, as he caressed her gentle lips. "Oh, yes, go, go, go . . ." Darlene gasped as her torso twisted and turned, her voice gathering strength, rising to a half scream as her hand scrambled to grasp his pulsating warmth. "Now, now, now, oh, God, now!" she yelled, pulling on him, leading him into her honeyed chamber. As their exploration of ecstasy quickened in pace, her thighs rose up and clasped around him. Little noises shot from her, sounds of absolute pleasure as she hugged his face to her breasts. She kept up with him, surging, twisting, thrusting, trying to let every inch of her body share in the fervent ecstasy.

He found her lips, and pressed down on them hard, seeing her opaque eyes staring at him out of some unfathomable depth of blue fire, a quality and an expression he had never seen before in anyone's eyes, as if she were experiencing pleasures from outside herself. With almost an angry insistence, she pulled his lips down to her breasts, pushing one eager mound into his mouth. Her pelvis rose again, thrusting upward as she gasped. He gave every part of himself, stroking her deliciously sensitive lips, sliding slowly, then faster, as he felt her body begin to quiver. She clung to him, arms, legs, and belly pressed hard into him, her screams rising, spiraling, anticipating that moment forever new and forever old, when the world ceased to turn for that single explosion of intimate ecstasy.

He felt his own response rising with her, matching her flaming, frantic wanting. Her cry erupted, a shriek of pure ecstasy as her body trembled violently, seeming to hold in midair until, with a cry of anger and despair, passion culminated in its own special, almost mocking way, as the taste of infinite pleasure was made terrible, finite. "Damn, god-damn," he heard her hiss as she fell back on the bedroll, falling instantaneously limp. He peered at her and saw that her eyes had lost their wild intensity, returning to their masked opaque blue.

"It never lasts long enough," he said as her lips stayed tight. She gave a tiny, wry snort of agreement, her mouth softening.

"You'd know better than I," she answered with an

edge of tartness, pulling him against her, keeping his chest tight against her breasts. "I'm glad for tonight, Fargo," she said. "It made us closer. Now you'll see me not just as somebody who hired you, but somebody who needs you."

"It's always nice to be needed," he said. "How's Jody?"

"Sulking," Darlene said. "I've guards around the house. She won't be running off again." Reaching for her jeans, Darlene started pulling them on. "I don't want to be seen coming back at dawn. We'll find other times and other places when you get back." The thought definitely appealed to Fargo yet he marveled at how quickly she could put away the fire and leave only ice, her patrician face now entirely composed, as if nothing had happened but minutes ago.

"I've a question," he asked. "What if your pa doesn't want to come back with me?"

"I don't expect he will. Don't make an issue of it," Darlene said. "You just hurry back and tell me where you found him. I'll do the rest." He nodded as she pulled herself onto the gray gelding. "I'll be anxiously waiting to hear from you," she said, "for more than one reason." Her smile was a flash of promise before she rode off and vanished into the darkness. He lay down to sleep for the rest of the night in the little arbor, his plans for the morrow already in place.

4

Morning rode in on a hot sun and Fargo woke with
his mood dark as he bathed in a brook. He'd been
awakened during the night by the sound of wolves,
three different packs and all too close. But he hadn't
been surprised. Wolves were thick in this heavy timber country, which was perfect for hiding, tracking,
and bringing down their quarry. When he finished
washing, he rode leisurely, searching the land without really expecting to find anything. The man he
had been tailing until Jody interrupted him had had
more than enough time to return, pick up his trail,
and go on. Trying to find his prints would be un-
productive. But chickens always came home to
roost, so Fargo waited until night fell, and made his
way back to Hightop, taking up a position in the
deep shadows between two sheds.

From this spot, he could watch the door of the saloon and as the hours dragged on, his eyes stayed
fastened on it as only loggers weaved their way into
the night. The ordinary man would have grown impatient and made the wrong move, but Fargo
waited as the eagle waits, knowing that sooner or
later its prey would come into sight. Finally, the

sounds of the saloon grew still as the last of the customers staggered out. But one horse remained at the hitching post, Fargo noted. It was but a few minutes more when the man he had been tracking appeared, the madam beside him. He had a somewhat flabby face, Fargo saw, getting his first proper look at him, a thick upper lip adorned with a small mustache, his stomach carrying a slight paunch. He exchanged a few more words with Dolly and when the madam returned to the saloon, he took his horse and rode from town. Not in a galloping hurry this time, but at a slow trot.

Fargo hung back until the man was out of sight, then he moved from the shadows and followed after him, staying back just far enough to pick up the slow pattern of hoofbeats. The rider turned west this time, and as Fargo followed he came to a fairly steep incline. He slid from the pinto and led the horse up the slope, listening to the man ahead keep his horse at a walk, then finally come to a halt. Fargo stopped and held one hand on the Ovaro's snout as he listened. There were no more hoofsteps. The rider had dismounted, and Fargo slowly moved up the slope, noting the incline level off and the little cabin at the top where the land grew flat. Moving into the red cedar at the borders of the incline, he crept forward and saw lamplight shine from the one window of the cabin.

As he drew closer, staying inside the cedars, he saw a lean-to at the back of the cabin where the horse had been tied, as well as the handle of a small well a dozen feet away, a cord of wood, and a closed feedbox. This was no way station. The man lived there permanently. Draping the reins of the pinto over a low branch, Fargo went on himself, his steps silent as a cougar on the prowl. The man had left the door ajar and was undressed, down to his trousers and undershirt. Fargo reached the door, drew his Colt, and pushed into the room, a single square with a cot along one wall. The man looked up, his flabby face widening.

"Surprise," Fargo said as the man's eyes went to the Colt aimed at his midsection, shifting to his own gun hanging at the corner of the cot. "Don't do anything stupid," Fargo said mildly. "You have a name?"

"Harry," the man muttered, glowering at his visitor.

"Well, Harry, you have a choice," Fargo said.

"Like what?" the man said.

"Like staying alive or dead," Fargo said. "Where's Bill Tillman?"

"I don't know," the man growled.

"Lying can get you dead," Fargo said. "Dolly sent you after him. Where'd you go?"

"No place," Harry said stubbornly.

"Wrong answer. You get one more chance."

"Killing me won't get you Bill Tillman," the man said.

"You're right but it'll stop you from delivering messages," Fargo said. "Where is he?"

"Go to hell," the man said, surprising Fargo. Harry didn't seem the selfless, loyalty-over-survival kind. He had to be awfully afraid of something.

Fargo saw the man's lariat hanging from the end of the cot. "Turn around, Harry," he said as he stepped forward, taking the lariat and holding the Colt into the man's back as he wrapped the rope around his wrists. He then pushed Harry facedown on the cot. Working quickly, Fargo tied the man hand and foot, each knot strong and tight. "I'm going to give you a chance to get smart, Harry," Fargo said. "I'll be back in the morning. You be ready with answers then, or else." Harry's face stayed resolutely set but Fargo knew how quickly time could corrode the most dedicated of men. "Tomorrow, Harry. Last-chance time," Fargo said as he walked from the cabin and closed the door behind him. He returned to his horse, rode down the incline, and found a place to bed down in a nest of Engelmann spruce.

He slept, awakened only once by the howling of wolves, and he had just finished washing in the morning sun when he heard the rumble of hoofbeats. He swung onto the pinto, and peered through the trees to see at least a dozen horses. One led all the others, and he caught the glint of the rider's dusty blond hair. Fargo spurred the Ovaro forward and crossed in front of the riders as they reached an open area. Darlene reined up at once as he approached. "What's all this?" he asked her.

"Search party," she said flatly.

"Thought you hired me for that," Fargo said.

"Not for pa, for Jody. The little bitch got out and took off," Darlene said. "I want her back."

"Concerned over her?" Fargo asked mildly.

"I don't give a damn about her. I just want her out of my hair. I know she's out looking for her uncle."

"What difference does it make if she finds him?" Fargo questioned.

"God knows what she'll say. He listens to her. Finding him is none of her damn business. I don't want her interfering," Darlene said with icy anger.

"She's not likely to find him," Fargo told her. "She's more likely to get herself hurt, maybe killed. Should I try to find her?"

"No," Darlene snapped. "You forget about her. If we don't find her she can get herself killed. The hell with her." She snapped her reins and rode off, the twelve men following her north, where they spread out into the thick forests. When they were beyond sight, Fargo turned the Ovaro west. Darlene's answer to his question bothered him. It had been too vague, too glib for the kind of anger she spewed out, an anger resulting from more than simply a clash of personalities, as he had previously considered. He continued to send the Ovaro west, retracing steps. Harry could wait a little longer. He'd have more time to edge closer to a tongue-loosening panic.

When Fargo reached the hollow he slowed, led the horse into the trees surrounding it, swung from the saddle, and walked forward. When he reached the end of the hollow, he uttered a silent grunt in satisfaction, seeing the figure bending low, peering at the ground as she tried to locate hoofprints. He stepped to the edge of the trees. "Lose something?" he asked and Jody spun around, staring at him in disbelief as he stepped from the trees.

"Damn," she murmured.

"I knew you'd come here," he said.

"How?"

"You'd no place else to start looking," he said as she glared back. "Why do you keep running away, dammit?"

"I was scared," she said. Her pink blouse with a high, fluted collar made her face seem even younger than it was. She thrust her hands into the pockets of a full, gray skirt. "She made me a prisoner, kept me locked in my room. I think she's gone sort of crazy."

"I don't entirely figure Darlene," he admitted, thinking of her visit to him. "But she's not crazy. Complex, unusual, maybe really unsure of herself."

"Darlene unsure of herself? Ha!" Jody flung back, her brown eyes darkening. Fargo peered at her. Perhaps her fear of Darlene was unjustified, but it was real, he was convinced. She wasn't the kind for guile.

"All right, I won't take you back," he said. "You can string along until I find a safe place for you. Get your horse," he said and retrieved the Ovaro. She was already atop the brown gelding when he came alongside her, and he turned the pinto and headed for the little cabin.

"Where are we going?" she asked.

"To see a man," Fargo said.

"The one you were trailing when . . ."

"When you loused it up? That's right," Fargo growled. "This time I don't want to hear a word from you. Whatever I say, whatever I do, you be quiet."

She peered at him with her eyes very round. "You going to kill him?" she asked.

"That depends on him," Fargo returned. She looked away, blinking hard. "Sometimes when you put yourself into something you have to grow up fast," he said, not ungently.

"I guess so," she said, drawing herself in. He smiled inwardly. That combination of naiveté and determined stubbornness remained firmly in place. She stayed silent as they rode up the slope and the little cabin appeared at the top. Fargo went to the window and peered in before he pushed the door open. Harry looked up at him from the cot, bluster and anger mixed in his face.

"Ready to talk, Harry?" Fargo queried.

The man glanced at Jody. "Who's she?" he threw back.

Fargo decided that the less the man knew the more his tongue might reveal. "A man's got to have some relaxation," he said and saw Jody's eyes widen in surprise and disapproval. "I'm waiting," he said to Harry. "Where's Bill Tillman?"

Harry glanced away and didn't answer. Fargo decided to take a sidelong approach. "Dolly won't know you told me," he said.

"She'll know," the man blurted.

"You're awfully afraid of Dolly," Fargo observed.

"She'll tell Bill Tillman," the man threw back. "I don't aim to be crushed to death by logs, another accident that was no accident."

"Like the man I saw tied to a log?" Fargo questioned.

"That's right. It's his way to keep discipline," Harry said.

"Whose way?" Fargo pressed.

"Bill Tillman. He's got other ways, too. They work, all of them. Only a damned fool crosses Bill Tillman," the man said. Fargo cast a quick glance at Jody, and saw that she held her face expressionless.

"Why is Dolly so loyal to him?" Fargo questioned the man.

"He owns the saloon," Harry said. "She runs it but he owns it. It's her bread and butter."

"So she sent you to tell Bill Tillman I was looking for him and asking questions," Fargo said and the man stayed silent. "Where'd you meet with him?" Fargo pushed.

"Forget it," Harry muttered.

"I can't and I won't. I'm not playing games," Fargo said, his voice hardening. "Talk or you die right here on this cot. It may take a while but without food or water you'll surely shrivel up. Count on it."

"I talk and Bill Tillman kills me on a log. I don't talk and I die here on the cot. I'll take the cot," the man said.

Fargo swore under his breath. "Your choice," he snapped, motioning to Jody to follow as he strode from the cabin. Slamming the door shut behind him, he climbed onto the Ovaro and rode down the slope as Jody caught up to him.

"You really going to leave him there to die?" she asked.

"He's not important enough," Fargo said. "He won't die." Jody frowned back. "He's Dolly's messenger. He doesn't show up in a few days she'll send someone looking for him. He knows that. That's why he picked the cot. He'll wind up weak and hungry, but not dead."

"I'm glad," she said, her frown staying as she squinted at him. "What if he had been important enough?" she asked.

"I can't say. It could have been different. I don't play guessing games," he told her sternly. "That bothers you?"

"Yes," she murmured. "I guess I'm not ready for this kind of world."

"You learn anything else?" he asked her after a few minutes.

"Such as?"

"That maybe your Uncle Bill isn't the wonderful man you think he is?" Fargo slid at her.

Her lips tightened. "You going to believe what someone like that man says?" she countered.

"He was a man scared plenty. He knows the score and I saw some things for myself," Fargo said.

"Uncle Bill has more than one foreman. He could leave the disciplining to them. It could be their doing, not his," Jody said.

"Maybe." Fargo smiled. "You and Dolly."

"What's that mean?" Jody frowned.

"Same loyalty, different reasons," he said, putting the pinto into a canter and finally returning to where he had first lost Harry's trail. It took him almost an hour of searching but he finally picked up the single set of hoofprints driven deep into the soil when the man had raced away. The prints went west into the heavy logging country, Tillman country, and as he rode with Jody beside him, he decided to let her stay with him. Perhaps she'd have some influence on Bill Tillman if he were found, Fargo mused. He led the way through the towering forests of lodgepole pine, Douglas fir and ponderosa pine, along with stands of blue spruce. The day had slid into late afternoon when Fargo reined up and dismounted, his eyes on where the prints had halted beside a small arbor. He pointed to the other hoofprints that marked the ground as Jody slid from her horse.

"Two horses besides Harry's?" Jody said tentatively.

"Very good," Fargo said. "Harry met them here, stayed a spell, and then went his way." Jody's eyes traveled to the line of prints that went east by themselves.

"Then he didn't meet Uncle Bill," Jody said, a note of smugness in her voice. Fargo didn't answer as he climbed onto the pinto and began to follow the prints of the other two horses into the tall forests. Jody rode at his heels until he finally halted, the day having dipped to an end. "Why are you following these prints?" she asked.

"They're Bill Tillman's," he said.

"No. Uncle Bill was alone. These prints show two riders," Jody said.

"Two horses," Fargo corrected. "One rider."

Her smooth brow furrowed at him. "Why do you say that? You guessing?" she demanded.

"No," he said and pointed to where the two horses had gone around a thick blue spruce and then a lodgepole pine. "You see the way the prints of the second horse follow the first one around the trees?" he asked and she nodded. "You see anything special about them?" he pressed.

"Such as?" She shrugged.

"They never vary, never come a little closer, never hang back some. A second rider wouldn't do that. He'd close in some for a moment, fall back a little. A second rider would never stay in exactly the same place," Fargo said as she frowned back. "Those are the prints of a packhorse being pulled along at the same pace, around every tree." Jody stared at the prints, her brow now deep with creases. "Bill Tillman," Fargo said.

She lifted her eyes to him. "I didn't see him with a packhorse that night," she said.

"I'd guess he already had it waiting somewhere for him," Fargo said.

Jody's eyes studied him. "I know now why Darlene hired you," she said.

"That sounds suspiciously like a compliment," Fargo said blandly.

"It might just be," Jody said. "You bothered by compliments?"

"I'm bothered by being hit from behind," he said. She came to him, putting her hands on his chest.

"I'm sorry for that. Can you forgive me?" she said.

"Guess so," he said, wishing she didn't look so young and trusting, the pink blouse pushing out from her womanly curves. He glanced up as the dusk began to settle. "Let's find a place to bed down," he said and she followed as he swung onto the pinto. When a thicket of wild plum trees appeared, he halted, unsaddled the Ovaro, and set out his bedroll. Jody took her bag and went deeper into the thicket. When she returned she wore a short nightgown that showed her nicely curved calves and smooth knees that echoed the roundness of her cheeks. With her open earnestness, she could reach out with a very womanly essence, he noted with growing awareness. In the short nightgown that clung to her, she was a beguiling combination. Jody took a beef strip from her bag and shared it with him as the night stayed warm and humid.

When he undressed to his shorts he felt her eyes on him, and as he stretched out on the bedroll beside her he caught her faintly musky scent. "What are you going to do if you find Uncle Bill?" Jody asked.

"Tell him his daughter sent me, that she's concerned about him," Fargo said.

"What if he says he doesn't care?"

"I'll go back and tell Darlene where I found him. She's mostly interested in knowing that he's all right," Fargo answered.

"I want to talk to Uncle Bill," Jody said.

Fargo thought for a moment. "Can't see any harm in that. It'd be only natural if you're there," he said.

"You saying I won't be?" she snapped.

"No. I'm saying you never know what happens," he said soothingly. She accepted the answer after a moment, and lay back to settle herself. "Get some sleep," he muttered as he closed his eyes. He felt her hand come around his arm, a soft touch resting on his biceps.

"Thanks for taking me along," she said.

"Didn't plan it. It just happened," he said. "So far."

"There's something to be said for honesty," she remarked.

"Go to sleep," he growled again.

"Yes, sir," she said tartly, and shifted herself to be more comfortable on the bedroll. But her hand stayed on his arm, he noted. As the night grew still he found sleep for himself. The night was deep when he awoke to a cougar's scream curling through the air. Jody was up and hard against him at once, clinging to him.

"Easy," he murmured as he held her, feeling the warm softness of her pressing into his chest. She refused to relax until the cougar's screams died out and the big cat went its way. When she pushed from him, he saw the tiny points pressed against the nightgown, her fear another kind of arousal.

"Sorry," she said. "Memories, too soon, too close."

"It'll never go away," he said. "Once you've heard the cougar's scream it stays with you always. Now, get back to sleep," he said and stretched out on the bedroll. Suddenly she was tight against his side, one arm draped across his chest.

"Just a few minutes more," she murmured and he lay awake until he heard her slide into sleep, felt her body relax against him. When the morning came to wake him, she had moved, but only a few inches. He rose and looked down at her. She slept with her arms folded across her breasts, her legs drawn up, a little-girl neatness to her. But the nightdress had pulled up to reveal beautiful thighs, full yet supple, very womanly. He was at his saddlebag when she woke, instantly pulling the nightdress down and rubbing sleep from her eyes.

"There's a brook a few yards on," he said and she

nodded as he strolled away. She waited until he'd finished. When he returned, she had a towel over one arm, looking very much like a little girl again. He gathered wild plums while she washed and they breakfasted on the sweet fruit before he led the way west into high logging country. He rode through deep cuts in the land where mountainsides of western white pine, blue spruce, Engelmann pine, and Douglas fir rose in towering beauty. He spotted a half-dozen lakes, some with logs piled behind giant splash dams. The terrain was as rugged as it was beautiful, and they were still deep in the lush forest as the day began to move toward dusk. So far he had seen the evidence of logging activity but nothing else. The forests were strangely silent, when suddenly the sound erupted.

It began high on the mountainside, filling the forest with a strange combination of whistles and roars, an unnerving noise that quickly grew louder, becoming an ear-piercing shriek. "My God, what's that?" Jody called out, alarm in her voice. He didn't answer but motioned for her to follow as he put the pinto into a canter, and followed a path along the lower part of the mountain. The whistling, roaring sound grew still louder, shaking trees, until it abruptly ended with a shattering impact, accompanied by the sound of a giant splash. Fargo pushed through a group of cedars, reined to a halt, and pointed to a long wooden V-shaped chute, fashioned of log sides with a shallow bed of water flowing along the bottom.

Almost six feet deep, it disappeared into the high reaches of the mountainside and ran out of sight as it slanted downward. "There," Fargo said. "It's called a flume." He'd just spoken when the roaring sound began again high up the mountainside. It quickly gathered strength, becoming the wild whistling din they had first heard. He saw Jody's eyes grow wide as a log appeared, hurtling down the V-shaped flume. Buoyed by the water at the bottom of the chute, the huge log passed by at breakneck speed, going so fast that smoke curled up from the friction the log created as it raced by. In seconds, it disappeared from sight down the chute and, moments later, a tremendous impact exploded as the log slammed into a lake or river. "It's said they go as fast as ninety miles an hour," Fargo said. Less than a minute later, another log roared its way down the flume, passing them with its huge, round form looking as though it were some wild apparition rather than a giant log.

"My God," Jody breathed and Fargo was still staring at the chute as another voice broke into his thoughts.

"Don't move, mister," it said. Fargo turned in the saddle to see men come out of the trees, eight of them, he counted, all carrying rifles aimed directly at him. The one who had spoken was tall and angular of body, had a slab-sided face and a prominent nose, with unruly black hair crowning his head. He drew closer while the others formed a circle around Fargo and Jody. "When are you Stenson boys going to learn?" he said.

"Learn what?" Fargo said.

"To stay off Tillman land," the man said with a growl.

"Is this Tillman land?" Fargo asked.

"You know goddamn well it is. Don't play innocent with me. Nobody plays Charlie Durkin for a fool," the man said.

"Wasn't trying to do that, Charlie," Fargo replied, keeping his tone bland.

"You've your nerve, bringing your chippie here," Charlie snapped.

"You've got it all wrong, Charlie. First, I'm not one of Stenson's boys," Fargo tried.

Charlie's angular face broke into what might have been a smile. "The hell you're not. We know that Stenson lets his boys keep women. You think we'll let you go because you brought her?"

"She's Bill Tillman's niece," Fargo said.

Charlie burst out in a guffaw that the others joined in on at once. "And I'm the Queen of England," he roared. One of the others stepped forward, a short, stout figure wearing a wide logger's belt with its hooks and buckles for attaching various equipment.

"Take your gun out, mister, real slow. Throw it on the ground." Fargo eyed the circle of rifles aimed at him. His draw was fast enough to bring down at least half of them, but that would set off a return fusillade from the others. Jody was directly in the line of fire, certain to be hit. He cursed under his breath as he lifted the Colt from its holster, and let it drop to the ground. One of the men darted forward, scooped up the gun, and handed it to Charlie. "Get off your horse," the man commanded. "You, too, girlie."

Fargo dismounted, and saw Jody swing to the

ground. Two of the men seized her at once. "You're making a big mistake," Fargo said.

"No, you made the mistake, but you're not the first one," Charlie said, calling into the trees. Four more men appeared, each holding a rifle as they shepherded three prisoners in front of them. "These are three more of Roy Stenson's boys we caught on Tillman land. They were carrying dynamite on their way to blow up one of our dams," Charlie said. Fargo glanced at the three men who stared sullenly at the ground.

"We're not carrying anything and we're not Stenson's people," Fargo said.

"Doesn't much matter. We'll show you what happens to anybody on Tillman land without permission," the man said just as the whistling roar started high up on the mountainside, and began to gather instant power. He pointed to one of the three prisoners. "Start with him," he ordered. Four of the guards seized the man, lifted him from the ground, and threw him into the flume.

"No, Jesus, no!" the man screamed as he hit the bed of water inside the chute. He tried to rise and scramble over the edge of one slanting wall but then slipped, fell, and tried to pull himself up again. But it was impossible, Fargo saw, the sides of the chute were too wet and slippery, the bottom covered with water that allowed him no footing. The clamor filled the air now, as the man in the chute desperately tried to climb out, his fingers clawing at the wet sides of the V-shaped flume, only to slip off helplessly. "Help me, Jesus, help me," he screamed. One of the other prisoners took a step toward the flume, but a rifle butt knocked him to the ground.

The man in the chute fell to the bottom again as he slipped from the smooth sides and Fargo saw his eyes widen in abject terror. The hurtling log came into view, rushing down the flume with the speed of a runaway locomotive. The terrible sound drowned out the man's scream and in a split second the huge log smashed into him at full force. Fargo saw the air turn red as sprays of scarlet rose upward, and he was grateful that the roaring sound drowned out the crunch of a human body being smashed into bits. Suddenly Jody was against him, arms wrapped around him, her face buried into his chest as she trembled, tiny sounds falling from her lips. Mercifully, Fargo saw, the hurtling log carried whatever remained of the man with it as it raced down the chute, leaving only a few streaks of red in the water and on the sides of the flume. The loud impact of the log as it hit the water broke the spell of awe and horror that Fargo felt sweep through him and Jody pushed back, turning to glare at Charlie. "You sick monster," she bit out, her voice tight. "You horrible, rotten, sick brute."

The roar began again from high on the mountain. Charlie pointed to another of the two remaining prisoners. "He's next," he said. The man screamed as he was lifted and thrown into the flume. Fargo started to advance toward the chute and saw the rifles swing around at him. The third prisoner lay on the ground, his hands clasped together in prayer and Fargo's eyes went to the figure inside the chute. Like the man before him, he scrambled and clawed to escape but there was no place he could get hold of on the smooth sides of the chute. He, too, slipped and fell and tried to clamber out again, only to fall back. Fargo felt Jody against him once again, her body trembling, her face buried into his shoulder.

The roar, now a scream of impending death, rose higher and the huge log flew down the chute. Fargo's face drew together in fury and helplessness as the log smashed once again into the figure in the chute. The man's scream somehow managed to rise over the din of the hurtling log, cut mercifully short but once again, the terrible spray of scarlet plastered the flume and the air. It was all over in seconds, the log hurtling on its way, leaving only a few streaks of red behind as it obliterated the figure in front of it. "My God, oh my God," Jody murmured against Fargo. Turning to look at Charlie again, she gasped. "Monster, monster, monster!" But Charlie was already lifting the third prisoner to his feet.

"You can find your way back to Roy Stenson. Tell him what happens to his boys when they come onto Tillman land," Charlie said and Fargo saw the man, his face pale as a new cotton sheet, turn and begin to run off, crashing his way through the trees. Charlie turned to face Fargo, Jody still against his side. The man wore a smug expression on his angular face. "Now, that's how to send a message," he said.

"Bastard. Monster!" Jody screamed, and started to fly at Charlie but Fargo grabbed her arm and yanked her back.

"Real little spitfire, isn't she." Charlie laughed. "I like that. She'll be fun to tame."

"She's Bill Tillman's niece, I'm telling you," Fargo said.

The man's eyes narrowed at him. "I don't believe a damn word of that. Who're you, his cousin?" Charlie said.

"No, but she's his niece," Fargo insisted.

Charlie laughed again. "Bullshit. You're one of Stenson's boys come in here with a fancy story," he said.

One of the others broke in. "Hold on, Charlie. You know we heard there was somebody out tracking Bill Tillman. Maybe he's the one," the man said.

Charlie's eyes narrowed at Fargo as thoughts plainly sifted through his head. "That might just be," Charlie said. "Is that who you are, mister?"

"Take me to Bill Tillman and find out," Fargo said.

Charlie threw his head back in a coarse laugh. "You'd like that, wouldn't you? You must think I'm a damn fool," he said. "Bill Tillman doesn't want to be found."

"Why not?" Fargo snapped out quickly.

"I don't know and you won't be finding out," the man said, his eyes greedily moving over Jody.

"Leave her be. She's just tagging along with me," Fargo said.

"Well, then we'll be taking real good care of her," the man said.

Fargo's eyes flicked upward. Dusk was settling in over the mountains. Dark would come if he could hold out for another ten minutes, dark that would give him a chance to make a break for it. "Tillman's on the run, isn't he?" Fargo asked to keep the man talking. "He running from Roy Stenson?" Fargo pressed.

"Maybe yes, maybe no. Might be he just wants to lay low," Charlie said.

"He has to have a reason," Fargo said as dusk deepened. But the whistling roar suddenly erupted again from high on the mountain. Charlie nodded and four of the men seized Fargo before he had a chance to set himself but he still managed to double up one with a blow to the stomach. But the others had him and he felt himself thrown into the flume. He heard Jody screaming as he hit the bottom of the chute, and he pushed himself onto one knee and tried to claw his way up the side. But he found out he could do no more than any of the others had. There was no way to climb out. There was only wet, slippery wood. Jody was still screaming when a hard slap stopped her.

But nothing stopped the roar from growing louder, filling his ears until he thought they would burst. The last trace of dusk was descending but he knew he'd never see it if he were in the flume another twenty seconds longer. Trying again to climb out was useless, he realized. The sides of the chute were too smooth, too slippery. He thought of letting himself slide down the chute but knew that would only delay his crushing demise by another few seconds. On one knee in the shallow water at the bottom of the flume, he reached down and pulled the double-edged knife from its calf holster around his leg. He pushed to his feet just as death came into sight, hurtling toward him through the darkness, its whine a wild cry of final triumph.

5

Death and darkness were descending on him quickly, and Fargo knew that hurtling, obliterating, pulverizing death would win the grim contest. He pushed himself to his feet, turned away from the side of the chute where the others waited, raised the knife, and using every ounce of his strength, drove the blade into the slanted side of the flume. It pierced the wood easily, stopping only when the hilt would let it go no deeper. He felt the flume shake as the massive projectile raced at him. It screamed, a bone-rattling screech that demanded to be looked at. But Fargo refused, knowing that to do so would be to be caught in its spell, as a rodent is transfixed by a rattlesnake's stare. His last few seconds of life would be frozen by the face of death.

Keeping his eyes on the knife imbedded into the side of the flume, he curled his hand around the knife handle. It held rock-firm as he leaped, swinging himself up, using the knife handle to provide a grip the slippery sides of the chute had refused to offer. Flinging himself upward, he catapulted his body over the top edge of the chute. He felt the tremendous rush of wind as the hurtling, screaming log grazed his foot and then he was on the ground, picking himself up and starting to run as the darkness descended. The huge log had passed, racing its way on down the chute and he heard shouts from the other side of the device. The shots erupted next but he was running, darkness a welcome shroud.

The combined rifle fire became a withering fusillade, bullets spraying in a wide pattern, smashing into the ground and trees on all sides of him. A rifle bullet struck him along his rib cage, not a direct hit yet powerful enough to send him sprawling face forward to the ground. He lay for a minute, felt the blood streaming from between his ribs, and he cursed as he pushed to his feet. Fighting away the sharp stab of pain, he began to run again as more shots thudded into the trees all around him. He had managed to run another dozen yards when one more of the spraying bullets found him, this one a downward trajectory that caught his leg.

He gasped at the bullet's sharp sting and was grateful as he felt it tear through his leg and come out the other side of the fleshy part of his thigh. Blood immediately poured down his leg as pain shot up along his left side. He turned, plunged into a row of cedars, and heard the last volley of shots fade away. But he knew it wasn't finished. There had to be a place nearby where the flume was elevated enough for them to duck underneath. They'd head for it on the run, he was certain, and come searching for him, hoping fervently that they had been lucky, that one of their volleys had brought him down.

He cut through the cedars, slowed by racking

pain that now consumed his entire body. In the first light of the rising moon, he spied a solid stand of butterweeds surrounding the base of the cedars. Standing almost six feet tall, the butterweeds offered a densely curtained hiding place, with stalks and stems that were both delicate yet strong. Best of all their stalks sprang back into position almost immediately. He edged his way through the thick mass of the butterweeds and sank to the ground amidst them, disappearing inside their thick density. He lay there, his lips pulled back in a grimace as the throbbing pain in his body increased. He didn't need to lift his head to hear the footsteps draw near. Fargo listened as his pursuers passed near, certain he had run in a straight line. They moved on but he stayed motionless, resting his head on one arm and cursing at the blood that was oozing from his ribs and leg.

Fargo fought away the waves of nausea that swept over him and knew that weakness would soon be his main problem. He guessed another half hour had gone by when he heard the men returning. Fargo let his ears be his eyes, and figured they were still spread out, still searching for him. The moon had come up but the cloak of butterweed blanketed him, its intertwined stalks forming a solid curtain. He listened to their footsteps, which told him they were moving too quickly to find anything they didn't stumble directly over. They went on and after a while he heard the sound of horses from beyond the flume. They were leaving, taking Jody with them, of course. Fargo stayed a few minutes longer under cover of the butterweeds and knew he was too nauseous and dizzy to try and follow, the night making that almost impossible even if he'd had all his faculties.

Still, he shook away the pain and sat up, aware that the first thing he needed to do was to staunch the flow of blood. He stripped off his shirt, retied it as tight as he could around his ribs, and used the sleeves to wipe away some of the warm, sticky blood that covered his side. In moments, he felt the flow of blood slow, as the pressure of the tied shirt held it in place. His thigh came next and fighting off intense pain again, he removed a boot and used his sock to make a tourniquet just above the wound. Again, the flow of blood lessened immediately, so he pulled the boot back on and rose to his feet. Pushing through a wave of dizziness, he made his way from his butterweed sanctuary. Once out of the weeds, the moonlight brought its pale glow to the forest and as he moved forward, Fargo saw the tall rounded cylinders of huge tree stumps left after the trees had been felled, amidst the towering forest giants that were still to be cut down.

He saw that a number of these had long pieces of flat wood extending horizontally from their tops some six to eight feet from the ground. Springboards, they were called, hammered into the trees to give the loggers a place to stand as they chopped into the forest giants above the base trunks that were too thick and swollen to chop into cleanly. He also caught sight of other objects beside the trees—broadaxes, bucking saws, falling axes with their double blades, ten-foot crosscut falling saws, and cans of lubricant. Loggers plainly preferred leaving the heavy equipment to lugging it back and forth. Fargo moved on, slowly, favoring his weakened, pain-riddled body and he'd gone another hundred yards when his ears first picked up the sound of softly padding footsteps, then the almost noiseless exhaling of breath.

He halted, automatically reaching for his gun and cursing as his hand felt only the empty holster. The long, soft panting sounds came again and he slowly turned his head to the right, already certain of what he'd find. Yellow eyes speared back at him and he counted six pairs of the penetrating, baleful orbs. He glanced to his left, and found another four pairs of eyes. In the distance, further back in the trees, he spied at least three more pairs. He moved backward, and began to retreat toward the towering cedars as two of the yellow eyes moved with him. As the eyes came closer, the form of a long-legged, gray timber wolf took shape. Two more wolves came forward and Fargo, ignoring the pain that shot through him with each step, began to trot toward the trees. A quick glance showed him the wolves splitting into two groups, one on each side of him.

One moved closer, his gray coat almost black, trotting a few feet in front of the others, plainly the pack leader. Fargo maintained his quickened pace but saw the wolves edging closer. They had arrived quickly, drawn by the scent of fresh blood, Fargo knew, the blood that still lay caulked on his body. With their pack instinct, the wolves would know the right moment to attack their prey, the moment when weakness invited the first slash of those killing fangs. Fargo cursed as he tried not to stumble, grimacing with pain. At least ten pairs of yellow eyes were watching him, gauging, probing with their instinctive security that would tell them when to strike. They would not make a mistake. They never did.

There was no deceiving them, Fargo thought, and he saw the gray shapes almost soundlessly move in closer. They were responding to the messages they picked up, the scent of weakness, the signs of vulnerability. Fargo knew that he'd have no chance on the ground, where every advantage was theirs. He broke into a run, pain shooting through his body with every step. The wolves immediately went into their long lope, moving as if one, still edging closer. A big cedar loomed up ahead of him and Fargo saw the springboard extending out from its trunk, a bucking saw and a broadax lying on the ground in front of the tree. He reached the huge trunk, scooped up the bucking saw and saw one of the wolves charge from the pack, its body flattening as it raced toward him. He raised the saw in both hands, dug his heels into the ground and forced himself to face the long fangs that rushed at him.

The wolf leaped directly at him and Fargo half crouched, bringing the big saw upward as if it were a warrior's shield, and the wolf slammed into it. Fargo was knocked backward but not before he saw the spurting line of blood that came from the animal's throat. Falling to the ground, the wolf half cried, half choked as it collapsed to one side. But the charge had triggered the others and Fargo saw two gray shapes coming at him from the other side. This time he swung the big saw in a half arc, its sharp, jagged teeth slicing into one of the two attackers. The wolf yelped in pain as it curled and fell away. The second wolf turned aside with a skidding, flinching motion of its body as Fargo saw the pack leader circling to come in from the other side. Turning, Fargo raced for the springboard protruding from the big cedar.

He felt the rush of warm breath on the back of his neck as he flung himself into a dive. The great, gray form sailed over his head, teeth snapping on empty air. Fargo rolled, came up on his feet, twisted away from another leaping form, and scooped the broadax from the ground. Blocking out the wave of pain that went through him, he leaped into the air. Unable to keep his hold on both tools, he dropped the saw and maintained his grip on the broadax as he got one arm over the edge of the springboard. He managed to pull himself up onto the narrow, flat board as his calf felt the pain of raking fangs that just missed sinking in deeply. He drew his legs up, paused for a second and then pushed to his feet just in time to see another wolf leap up to the board from the other side.

The animal had both front paws over the board, and was beginning to pull himself up further when Fargo swung the broadax at the thick forepaws. The wolf yelped in pain as it fell backward and plummeted to the ground. Fargo waited, the broadaxe raised, ready for the next leaping attacker. But there was none. Instead, he heard the sounds of snarling, tearing, and ripping from below and, dropping to one knee, he peered over the edge of the springboard. As was their way, the pack was attacking the three bleeding and injured members, turning on the weak regardless of who and what they were. It was the wolf's code, instinctive, unchangeable, as ancient as the species itself. Their killing frenzy would last through the rest of the night and when they were finished, satiated, they'd go their way. That, too, was their way, he knew and he stayed in place, fighting off waves of weakness and resting on the narrow island of safety.

Hours passed, filled with the shredding, snarling sounds, until finally it was over, the silence so sudden it made its own statement. Fargo lifted his head and watched the gray shapes vanish into the forest as though they were wraiths disappearing into thin air. He didn't move, rather he put his head down again and let another hour go by before he lowered himself to the ground, his body protesting as he dropped the last few feet. He moved slowly, found a spot beside a huge western pine, and sank to the ground, closing his eyes and sleeping until dawn peeked through the trees. He rose, found a brook, and cleaned as much of the blood from himself as he could. When he went on, he knew that some of his strength had returned. Enough to keep going, anyway.

His eyes searched the forest as he moved forward. He returned to the flume, and when he crossed under it, he saw that Tillman's men had taken the Ovaro and Jody's horse with them. They made distinctive tracks, easy to pick up, two sets of hoof marks, set apart from the rest of the footprints, and he saw their trail go west. Fargo quickened his pace as he followed. He knew the area would soon be full of loggers picking up their tools to again attack the forest giants. Fargo fought down waves of pain that swept through him and continued to hurry, falling into a long, even stride that slowed only when he reached a part of the forest where the trees were untouched, where loggers were not at work. The trail turned, and led downward to where the land flattened into a great hollow equally covered with tall timber. He slowed and, peering through the trees, he glimpsed figures in a circle of quaking aspen. He crept forward, staying inside the heavy foliage of the aspen until he found Jody off to one side, tied to a sapling.

She seemed not much the worse for wear except for her hair, which hung disheveled in her face. Scanning the scene, he spotted the Ovaro and Jody's horse, then brought his eyes back to the eight figures, spotting the angular features of the one called Charlie. Some were still on the ground where they had camped for the night. "Tillman's gonna be busy for at least another two days," Fargo heard Charlie say to the others. "We've got some time to decide."

"I say we get rid of her before tomorrow," one of the others said. "Christ, what if she really is Tillman's niece?"

"You gonna believe what that big bastard said? He was trying to save his neck," Charlie said.

"Didn't say I believed him. Don't want to take any chances, either," the other man muttered.

"All right, she disappears in the river. Case closed, whoever she is," Charlie agreed.

"Not before we enjoy her," someone else said.

"Tonight," Charlie said. "We only got a few

hours' sleep. I want to be at my best for the little lady." He laughed, throwing a glance at Jody. Fargo's eyes narrowed as the eight figures gathered themselves, untied Jody, and put a rope around her neck as they set off, one leading the two horses. Fargo followed, staying close enough only to keep them in sight through the trees. He'd only get himself killed by a hasty attempt to reach Jody. He needed a weapon and that meant waiting for a chance to get one of them apart from the others. They continued to go west, through heavy forest, and Fargo saw the sun pass the noon mark in the sky, beginning its slow curve downward. It had reached late afternoon when Charlie pointed to a half circle of serviceberry against the towering growths of ponderosa pine behind them. They moved into the half circle, tied Jody to a tree, and settled themselves on the ground. Two stretched out near Jody, the others spread out leisurely. Fargo saw as he moved closer that they had tied the horses together to a low branch.

He swore under his breath. None of the men were far enough away from each other for him to strike without waking the others. He watched them settle down to sleep and decided to wait. Backing away from the spot, he spotted a long field of lupines, their soft purple flowers contrasting with the green foliage at the base of the ponderosa. Crawling into the tall lupines, he stretched out, closed his eyes, and slept through the rest of the day. He'd hear their voices the minute they woke, he knew, and he slept comfortably, his body welcoming the chance to restore itself again. The dark gray of dusk was about to turn into night when he snapped awake, the voices reaching his always sensitive hearing. Rising, he made his way back to the half circle of aspen, and saw the men had built a small fire. For light, not warmth. They wanted the pleasure of seeing as well as doing. They had taken the rope from Jody and two men held her by the arms, Charlie standing in front of her.

"You'll be sorry for this," Jody said.

"Don't you worry about us, girlie," Charlie said and turned to the others standing in a loose group behind him. "I'm first," he said and the others made no protest. He turned back to Jody, and started to walk toward her. When he was closer, she kicked out at him, a quick, supple movement. Charlie managed to twist away but the kick still caught him on his right hip.

"Bastards!" Jody spit at him.

"Damn," the man said, rubbing his hip. "Hold on to her, dammit. Take her down."

While the man were throwing Jody to the ground as the others guffawed in glee, Fargo crept still closer, stopping at the very edge of the aspen. The five men looking on had widened their half circle. One had stopped only a few feet from where Fargo crouched. He was the only one near enough to reach, Fargo saw, and even that would take perfect timing, speed, and not a little luck. But those were the only weapons he had, Fargo swore softly. He rose up, tightening the muscles of his legs despite the moment of pain that flared up at once.

They were all intent on watching Charlie as Fargo heard Jody's cries of fury and fear, seeing Charlie pulling her skirt off as the other two men held her. "Get a-goin', Charlie," one of the onlookers shouted. Fargo's eyes returned to the man nearest him. A tall, thin figure, he carried a six-gun in his holster and had put his rifle down on the ground beside him. Jody's screams rose and Fargo heard Charlie's voice as he rasped at the two men.

"Hold her still, dammit," he said.

Fargo straightened up. Their time was at an end. He sprang more than ran, leaving the foliage with the straight swiftness of an arrow. They hadn't heard him, their concentration all on Jody. His arm circled the man's neck at the same time as his other hand yanked the gun from the man's holster. The man had time only to utter a croaking sound before the gun crashed down onto his temple and he went limp. But it had been enough for the two men closets to him, who turned, surprise crossing their faces as they started to turn their rifles on him. They hadn't finished aiming when Fargo fired the gun in his hand and both men went down together. Another two spun at the shots, trying to bring their rifles up in time, but Fargo fired twice again, and both men flew backward at once to land in a heap.

Dropping to one knee, Fargo saw Charlie pull himself up from Jody, the two men holding her jumping to their feet, as well. Fargo fired the last shot in the revolver and one of the two men who'd been holding Jody pitched forward and lay still. Fargo dropped the pistol and scooped up the rifle as he rolled. Three shots landed where he had been. He fired from his stomach, almost flat on the ground. Charlie took the first two shots from the rifle, his body stiffening before it catapulted backward. The last man tried to run and fire at the same time and managed to do neither well. His shots were wild and he stumbled and almost fell. Fargo's shot helped him finish his fall.

Pushing to his feet, Fargo saw Jody had pulled her skirt up and came running toward him. She flew into his arms, and clung there for a long moment, her body shivering. "You're alive. Thank God," she murmured finally, drew back, her brown eyes searching his face, one hand pressing against his cheek. "I didn't know. You got out of the flume but they were shooting at you, and then they went after you," she said. "I asked when they got back and they said they'd taken care of you."

"They were hoping that," Fargo said. "Fact is, a pack of wolves came closer to doing that." A groaning sound cut into his words and he turned to see the first man he'd knocked out starting to sit up, one hand to his temple. Jody hurried beside Fargo as he strode to the man, who looked up, fear and pain in his face as he saw Fargo's rifle pointed at him. "You want to stay alive? Give me some answers. Bill Tillman has a main logging camp somewhere around here. Where is it?" Fargo demanded.

"I tell you and he'll kill me. That's for sure," the man said.

"You don't tell me and I'll kill you. That's for sure, too," Fargo said.

"I'll take a bullet over the flume, anytime," the man said. Fargo swore under his breath, even as he silently understood the man's decision. Yet he had to hold his ground, test the man's resolve to that final, ultimate moment.

"Your choice," he said, raising the rifle to fire.

The man licked his lips, the fear plain in his face. But his voice rose as he tried to summon courage. "You won't kill a man in cold blood. You're not the type. I've been around long enough to know. You won't, not with her looking on," he said.

"Looks are deceiving," Fargo said as he started to inch the trigger back.

"Wait!" the man cried out and Fargo relaxed the pressure of his finger on the trigger. "You've got to promise me you won't tell him I sent you," the man said and Fargo saw the craftiness shine in his eyes. It reflected a last attempt at bargaining for his life, Fargo decided.

"I won't tell him. My word on it," Fargo said.

The man drew a deep breath of relief. "Go south from here. You'll come to a high slope covered with blue spruce. Go up it and down the other side. The land levels out. Keep going south and you'll come to it. Three houses."

Fargo lowered the rifle. "Don't try following," he said. "You just bought staying alive. Don't push your luck."

The man nodded and Fargo stepped back, walking to where the two horses were tied together. He brought them to Jody, and handed her the reins of her mount while he stepped to where Charlie's body lay. He pulled the Colt Charlie had stuck in his belt and, his gun retrieved, swung onto the Ovaro. The survivor glowered up at him but stayed where he was. Fargo knew he'd not try to follow. His instincts for survival would govern his actions. Jody was already on her mount and swung alongside Fargo as he turned the Ovaro and rode from the spot into the almost pitch blackness of the forest night.

A moon filtered just enough light through the heavy tree cover to let them avoid colliding with the massive tree trunks that stretched in all directions. But he was certain they'd never find the slope of spruce in the night, Fargo told himself, and he rode on until, following a shaft of moonlight, he came to an arbor of serviceberry and butterfly weed. Even in the dark, the flaming scarlet of the butterfly weed kept its glow. "We'll bed down here till morning," he said, dismounting and unsaddling the Ovaro. Jody came over to him after unsaddling her mount and helped him lay out his bedroll as the moonlight played across the butterfly weed.

"What a lovely place. It's too bad we had to come onto it this way," she said.

"It's finding that counts, not how or why," he said. "Let's get some sleep." He waited while she got her things, expected she'd go behind one of the trees to change, but she didn't move. He saw her eyes grow wide as he shed his jacket and shirt.

"You're hurt," she gasped.

"I'm getting better," he said, pulling off his jeans, waiting again for her to retire behind one of the trees. But instead, she raised one hand and flicked open the buttons of her blouse, shrugged her shoulders, and the garment slipped from her. She pulled her skirt off, kicked it aside, and lifted the slip over her head, letting it fall to the ground. She met his eyes as he stared at her loveliness, took in her naked figure of surprising curvaceousness, every part of her smoothly flowing, shoulders, ribs, knees, elbows, not a bone angling out anywhere. His eyes lingered on two breasts so full and round they seemed to defy gravity. Small but very red nipples crowned each sweet swell, centered on modest areolas of deep pink.

A full rib cage added to the roundness of her, curving down to a slightly convex abdomen, and below it, the small outward curve of her belly, a deep indentation in the center somehow invitingly provocative. He followed the curve of her belly to where a full, dense little triangle pushed upward with an insouciance of its own. Below it, his eyes took in thighs that were lithe and limber as they tapered down to knees that were round and dimpled. He tore his eyes from her body and saw her soft brown orbs peering intently at him. "I'm surprising you," Jody said.

"Yes," he admitted.

"I'm surprising myself," she said, her smile almost reluctant.

His eyes narrowed on her. "You trying to say thank you?" he asked.

"Yes, but that wouldn't be enough," she said and he nodded. "There's more. It's called wanting," she added, coming forward and pressing herself against him, all warm softness. Her lips came to his, tentative for a moment, then turning bold. He responded, letting his tongue slide forward to touch and explore and Jody gave a sharp squeal of delight. He let his kiss grow stronger and deeper, and she didn't shrink back, her hands digging into his chest. He pulled back for a moment to search her eyes again.

"You sure?" he asked.

She nodded vigorously. "Very sure. Remember what you said when I told you maybe I wasn't ready for this world?"

He thought back a moment. "Yes," he recalled. "I said that sometimes, when you put yourself someplace, you have to grow up fast."

"You were right," she said and her mouth came to his again, pressing eagerly, opening to taste him, offering him her lips, her tongue, her moist warmth as she made little purring sounds. Her hands pressed against his chest and ran across his muscled pectorals. He felt himself responding to her smooth warmness, his hands encircling one perky breast, his thumb brushing across the red nipple. Jody cried out and he felt the little tip rise and grow firmer and he brought his mouth down to it, then gently drew it in. Jody's gasp was made of pure delight and she pushed her breast deeper into his mouth. He gently pulled on the soft mound, letting his tongue circle the areola, moving over the tip of her nipple, lingering, gently pulling. "Oh, God, oh, God, so good . . . oh, so good," Jody breathed.

His mouth stayed on her breast as his hand slid down over her convex little abdomen, then he caressed her small round belly, exploring, smoothing, painting with the brush of fiery senses. Jody cried out and he felt her hips turn upward, offering herself to him. He traced an invisible path further down, to the dense little triangle, pushing through her miniature downy forest, pressing to feel the rise of her Venus. He moved on downward, his hand sliding to thighs that were pressed together. Gently, he pushed forward and suddenly her thighs fell open, like a flower suddenly unfolding its petals to the sun. He felt the dampness, sweet harbinger and cry of silent sensuality as he moved further, and brought his hand to the dark portal. Gently, he probed forward, touching the infinite softness of lips that quivered. Jody's scream rose, echoing up to the very top of the great forest giants.

Her hips rose, surged upward, fell back, and then rose again. "Oh, my God, oh, please, please," she gasped, and he felt her hands hurrying down his own body, reaching for him, her scream a sharp mixture of alarm and pleasure. "Let me, let me, let me," she breathed and he moved his legs, let his pulsating warmth stand free for her, felt her hands close around him as she screamed again. She held him as he began to stroke, caressing her as her body twisted and turned, a kind of near panic in her movements, the kind of panic fueled by ecstasy beyond control. Little sounds came from her lips, half pleas, half demands, and he felt her pelvis lifting, turning, seeking, her hand pulling at him. He brought his hotness over her, and rested it on the dense triangle as Jody gasped out a shuddered cry. She drew her round little belly in and he felt her thighs fall open, clasping around him.

"Yes, yes, yes, please, please, please," she murmured and he moved, found her warm inviting portal and slid slowly forward, feeling the honeyed lips clasp around him in that embrace of all embraces.

Jody's cry echoed up into the forest, again and then again until it was one long wail of utter pleasure. Her belly rose, pushing against his as she surged with him, lifting, falling back, then rising up again. He felt the tightness of her around him and knew the meaning of the fervent embrace. But desire overwhelmed all else for her, ecstasy triumphing over every other emotion. Suddenly she was in charge, her torso writhing, twisting, surging, her cries now demands, her round, smooth body a temple of sensuous worship. He held her, surged with her, reveled in her discovery of pleasure and pleasure of discovery until suddenly he felt the soft warmness of her quivering against him. Arms, legs, breasts, belly, all of her quavering as she yelled out cries of deliverance from that almost unbearable pleasure.

He held her, rose with her, and exploded with her as she clung to him as a limpet clings to a rock. The sweet contractions flowed around him, her entire being, inner and outer, consumed with ecstasy received and ecstasy given. When the consummate moment devoured all else, as it always did, a tremendous shudder coursed through her and he heard her gasped cry of protest. Her legs grew limp around him, her arms relaxing their grip, but she stayed tight against him, her round breasts pressing into his chest. When she finally drew back, her eyes found his and he smiled at the expression he saw in her face. "It always happens. It's called disappointment," he told her.

"Too wonderful to end so quickly," she muttered.

"I didn't make the rules." He grinned. She pouted

as she pressed herself against him again. "Now, get some sleep," he said.

"Only if you promise," she said.

"Promise what?" he asked.

"To find another moment," she said.

"Promise," he said and she made a satisfied little sound, settling in against him. In moments he heard the steady sound of sleep coming from her lips. Her lovemaking had reflected her personality; a combination of naiveté, fresh eagerness, and surprising determination. Passion with none of Darlene Tillman's aggressiveness, he reviewed as he closed his eyes and found sleep with her. The night stayed warm and still and he slept soundly, waking only twice to the distant sound of wolves, until the new day's sun slowly filtered its way through the trees. He opened his eyes, enjoyed the warm touch of sun that came to rest on his chest, and looked at Jody. She had shifted during the night, her head now on his abdomen, her smooth thighs drawn up together and over his legs.

He had promised to find another moment and was tempted to make it happen then. But Bill Tillman waited not that far away, he reminded himself, and he tore his eyes away from her loveliness. First things first, he muttered to himself and she woke as he slid from under her. She sat up, still half asleep. "Time to move on," he told her and congratulated himself on his self-discipline.

6

They found a stream in which to wash and break-fasted on luscious mottled yellow and red wild plums. The slope of blue spruce took longer to reach than he'd expected, and it was only when they were going down the other side that he noticed Jody grow silent, her face drawing in on itself. "No sense in riling yourself up over it," he spoke at her as they reached the flatland at the bottom of the slope.

"Over what?" She frowned.

"Over meeting with your Uncle Bill," he said, catching the sharp glance she shot at him. "No sense in not seeing things, either," he said. She didn't answer. "He knows about putting men in the flume. You can't turn away from that anymore. No more blaming his foremen," Fargo said.

"Maybe he has to be hard. Maybe it's the only way he can protect himself, maintain discipline," she blurted out. He returned a skeptical glance. Her lips tightened and she looked away.

"It hurts," he said softly.

"What does?"

"Finding out somebody's not what you thought they were," he said.

"Yes," she said, her voice very small, not taking on strength. "But I haven't decided anything. Not till I know more. Maybe he's been forced into doing things. I want to know why he's run away."

"That makes two of us," Fargo said and backed away from pressing her further. He didn't have answers, either, he had to admit. But he'd get them, he promised himself, his thoughts suddenly turning to Darlene. She had seemed nothing other than a concerned daughter. But perhaps she knew things she hadn't mentioned. Or perhaps she knew things without knowing she did. He didn't discount that. The ice-fire blue eyes flashed through his mind, opposites wrapped together. A reflection of the opposites that were a part of Darlene? He wondered at the thought. She'd be more than impatient at not having heard from him, he was certain, as he peered forward through the stand of hackberry. But perhaps he was about to have the answer she wanted, Fargo told himself and put the pinto into a trot.

Jody beside him, he saw the hackberry grove begin to thin out somewhere when suddenly he reined the Ovaro to a halt. Jody shot a quick glance at him, starting to ask questions when he put one finger to his lips and she pulled her mouth closed. He pointed to the right and her eyes widened as she saw the sentry with a rifle in the crook of one arm. The man stood on a mound of earth that gave him a wider view of the forest. Fargo slid from the saddle, motioned for Jody to do the same, and came to her side as she dropped to the ground. "Stay here," he whispered, handing her the Ovaro's reins. "Keep watching." He left her, and moved through the forest on silent steps, slipping between trees, twisting his shoulders as he did so that not a branch moved, not a leaf rustled.

He circled behind the sentry, slowed, and felt the frown slide across his brow as he saw two more figures some hundred yards away, also sentries carrying rifles. One faced west, the other east, and Fargo dropped into a crouch as he neared the figure atop the mount, crawling closer. Neither of the other two sentries faced him but he'd have to be quick and quiet, he knew. Flattening himself, he began to crawl forward, moving through a solid stand of reddish-brown broomsedge. Inching his way, hidden in the three-foot high perennial, he crawled to within three feet of the sentry, and thought about confronting the man with the Colt aimed directly at him. He soon discarded the thought. The man had his rifle. He might elect to chance winning a shootout. Misplaced heroics, automatic reaction, plain bad judgment, any of them could leap up and shatter what Fargo needed most—silence.

Fargo's fingers slid along the ground and found a handful of loose bits of rock. He palmed the material and swinging his arm in a wide, flat arc, he flung the stones and watched them hit the ground beyond the sentry. The man spun at once, his back to the figure flattened in the broomsedge. Fargo leaped up, Colt in hand. He crossed the few feet in one long stride, and brought the Colt down on the sentry's head. He caught the man and his rifle as the sentry collapsed, then lowered him to the ground and pulled him from the mound. Rising up, he motioned to Jody to circle around to meet him. Using his fingers, he signaled for her to walk the horses, then saw her begin to make her way through the trees. He peered ahead at the other two sentries in the distance. Neither had seen or heard anything; both were still in place. He stayed low, waiting until he saw Jody come into view leading her horse and the Ovaro.

He rose and hurried to meet her, leaving the horses in the tree cover as he took his lariat, then returned to the still unconscious sentry. He tore a piece of the man's shirt off, used it as a gag, then bound the man hand and foot. "This will keep him quiet and in place after he comes to," Fargo said when he finished. He took the Ovaro and began to lead the horse down a slope, taking a long, wide route around the two other sentries. He stayed on foot as they moved forward, and was glad he did as he spied two more sentries. Progressing carefully, he halted every few yards to scan the forest and spotted another two sentries on guard but far apart, each surveying a different section of forest. "Uncle Bill has a lot of watchdogs," Jody murmured.

"Just what I was thinking, especially for a logging camp, even a main one," Fargo said, steering a path through a particularly heavy cluster of white pine. A stand of cottonwoods took over when the pine thinned and Fargo kept their careful, cautious progress as the day slipped into dusk. They had gone perhaps another half hour when he spotted the three houses as they came into sight, slightly back from the cottonwoods on partly cleared land. He felt the furrow cross his brow. There were three houses, as the man had said, but none were logging camp cabins. He saw a large main house of stone and logs, with a terrace along the front, stables and barns stretching behind it. To one side, a long bunkhouse stood, capable of holding at least thirty or forty men. A smaller yet still substantial bunkhouse was located behind it. Planted hedges around the main house further set it apart from a logging camp structure. Fargo crept another hundred yards closer, dropped to one knee, and peered through the trees at the main house.

Two guards flanked the house, one at each corner. In the growing dimness, Fargo saw a sign to one side, firmly fixed in the ground. His furrowed brow became a deep frown as he read the words painted on the square, wood sign:

PRIVATE PROPERTY
ALL VISITORS MUST STOP
AT MAIN HOUSE.
——ROY STENSON

"Damn," Fargo hissed as Jody came alongside him. "The son of a bitch sent us to the Stenson place."

"Why?" she breathed.

"It gave him time to get to your uncle and he probably expected we'd blunder in and get ourselves caught."

"Which would have happened except for you," Jody said. "Let's get out of here. Roy Stenson won't exactly welcome us."

"Not so fast. We've come all this way. I hate to see that go to waste," Fargo said.

"Meaning what?" she asked.

"Meaning Stenson might have some answers for us," Fargo said. "I'm going to find out what he knows and why he had Jimmy Donovan killed."

"All you'll do is get yourself killed," Jody said.

"Don't aim to do that," Fargo said. "It'll be dark in a half hour. I'll wait a little while longer and give Roy Stenson a surprise." He draped the reins of both horses over a low branch as Jody settled down beside him. Night descended and lights came on first in the bunkhouse, then in the main house. Fargo watched as the two sentries were replaced by a single guard who took up a position in front of the main entrance to the house. Fargo waited until the lamplight finally went out in the bunkhouse before turning to Jody. "Take your horse and get out of here if I don't come back in a half hour," he told her.

"I'm going with you," she said quietly.

"Hell you are," he said.

"Hell I'm not," she returned.

"It'll be tricky enough getting in alone," Fargo said.

"I won't get in your way. I'll just follow along. I can be as quiet as you can," she said.

"No you can't," he answered.

"Quiet enough. That's all that counts," she said. "What good am I going to do waiting? I'm here. I can help. You don't know what you'll find inside."

"I expect I'll find Roy Stenson," he said.

"Nevertheless, you don't know. I want to help. I've a stake in this, too, you know. Yours is money, to do your job. Mine's family," she said.

He frowned back, unable to deny the truth of her stand. She wouldn't fluster. She'd proven that. He let his frown vanish. "All right, but I call the shots. No questions, no debates," he said.

"Understood." She nodded and pushed to her feet with him. Fargo's eyes narrowed as he scanned the sentry in front of the door and the long sweep of the terrace that was open at both ends and along the front.

"Damn," he muttered. "There's no way to sneak up on him without him seeing us."

"Let him stay there. We'll go around to the back," Jody said.

Fargo shook his head. "He's too close to the door. He could hear something, raised voices, a shout, anything, and come busting in." He glowered into space for a moment longer. "I need a diversion to get to him. You." Jody's eyes turned to him, her brows lifting. "You're going to walk out, right at him," Fargo said. "But don't get too close. Let him come off the terrace toward you. Give me five minutes before you walk out. Get your story set while you're waiting." She nodded and he left her, staying in the cottonwoods as he moved to the side of the house, then halting opposite the end of the terrace. He had moved carefully, silently, and he estimated he'd used up almost three minutes as he stepped to the very edge of the trees.

Dropping to the ground, he began to crawl across the open land on his stomach until he neared the edge of the terrace. He raised his head just enough to let him peer along the terrace and the land in front of the house. Waiting, he saw the movement in the dark and then Jody appear out of the night, walking toward the house. The sentry saw her at the same moment, and straightened up as she came toward him. "That's far enough," he said, raising the rifle. Jody halted, a dozen feet from the terrace as the man stepped toward her. "Where the hell did you come from?" he growled.

"My horse foundered. I've been wandering, lost," Jody said. "I saw the house. Can you help me?"

"Who are you?" the guard questioned, suspicion filling his voice. "What the hell are you doing in this country?"

"I can explain," Jody said, coming a step closer and swinging her hips seductively. Fargo saw the guard's eyes take her in.

"Go on, explain," the man said. But his eyes were moving up and down Jody's shape. This was the moment, Fargo knew, the only one he'd have. He rose, ran silently on the balls of his feet, and crossed the few yards with the speed of a cougar's noiseless strike. The guard's attention was still completely riveted on Jody as Fargo's Colt smashed down on his head. He collapsed as Fargo snagged his rifle and tossed it to Jody. She caught it and came to him.

"Told you I'd be of help," she said smugly.

"You get a gold star," he said, stepping onto the terrace and halting at the front door. Closing his hand around the knob, he turned it slowly as the door opened with an almost inaudible click. He stepped into the house, Jody at his heels. A darkened living room opened up past the entranceway, but lamplight reached out from the room beyond. He crossed to the light and peered into the room to see a wood-paneled study. A man sat behind a heavy wood desk, a sheaf of papers spread out on the desktop. Fargo took in his salt-and-pepper hair, his beefy face with heavy brows and a short nose. His large head sat on a powerful shoulders. The man looked up as Fargo stepped into the room, surprise flooding his face. His hand immediately started to move toward the gun in the holster hanging over the back of the chair. "Don't even think about it," Fargo said quietly.

Roy Stenson saw the Colt pointed at his chest and put his hand back on the desk as his glance took in Jody. "What the hell is this?" he growled.

"Surprise visit," Fargo said.

"How'd you get past my man?" Stenson queried.

"Diversion," Jody answered. Stenson stared at her for a moment before returning his eyes to Fargo.

"You'll never get out alive, neither of you," he said.

"Let us worry about that, Stenson," Fargo said.

The man's eyes narrowed. "You know me. Let me know you," he said.

"Name's Fargo," the Trailsman said and Stenson thought for a moment.

"Fargo," he repeated. "You're the one looking for Bill Tillman," he said.

"Go to the head of the class. How'd you know?" Fargo asked.

"Word gets around," Stenson said. "He sure as hell isn't here."

"Where is he?" Fargo questioned.

"How the hell do I know? Checking his operation, I'd guess." Stenson grunted. "That's all I know."

"You know more, I think," Jody put in.

"I know he's one of the rottenest, stinking bastards this side of hell," Roy Stenson said.

"And you're a model citizen, of course," Jody said, her voice heavy with sarcasm.

"Didn't say that," Stenson answered. "But I don't put men in flumes to see them crushed to bits or tie them onto logs to arrange fake accidents."

"Gunning down a poor kid is all right, though," Fargo injected.

"What are you talking about?" Stenson frowned.

"You ordered Jimmy Donovan killed," Fargo said.

"Who's Jimmy Donovan?" the man returned.

"Cut the crap. He's the kid Darlene Tillman sent to find me but you had him killed," Fargo said.

"I didn't order Jimmy Donovan killed. Why should I?" Stenson asked.

"That's what I want to know," Fargo said.

"Why should I give a shit if Darlene Tillman sent for you?" Stenson snapped as Fargo's eyes bored into the man. Stenson seemed genuinely indignant. Fargo found himself wondering about the man's question. Why should Stenson care, he echoed and found no logical answer. Of course, that didn't mean there wasn't one. Stenson could be a convincing liar, he realized. But the question stayed with him as he faced the man.

"Maybe you're lying and maybe not but I'll find out. You're coming with us," he said.

"Where?"

"To show us the way to Bill Tillman's main logging camp. I'm sure you know where it is," Fargo said.

"I'm not going onto Tillman land. It'd be like signing my own death warrant," Roy Stenson said.

"You telling me you've never been on Tillman land? I'm not swallowing that," Fargo said.

"In my own time and my own way," Stenson said. "But I'm not being served up like a sacrificial lamb."

"I'll see that nothing happens to you," Jody said.

"What makes you think you can do that, girlie?" Stenson threw back.

"I'm his niece," Jody said.

Stenson gave a derisive snort. "You think that's going to mean anything to Bill Tillman? Shit, you don't know much," he said.

"He'll listen to me. We've a very warm relationship," Jody said.

"Enough of this. Get your horse," Fargo cut in and jabbed the Colt into Stenson's ribs. "We go out the back way." Stenson started from the room and Fargo kept the Colt against his back as they left through the rear door of the house. At the stable, Stenson saddled a good-looking roan, and started to mount. "Walk him," Fargo said, stepping in quickly, and led the way to where the Ovaro and Jody's horse waited. They walked the horses until they were far enough from the house to mount. Fargo stayed behind Stenson, Jody beside him. "One wrong move and you're gone," he warned Stenson as they started. He almost allowed a grim smile to touch his lips as they rode. The darkness didn't bother Stenson as he moved through the forest. It was plain he knew his way.

They'd ridden perhaps an hour when the first

streaks of dawn touched the sky. When they reached the top of a low slope, the land flattened and became a high tree-covered plateau. The dawn light quickly grew stronger and Fargo saw they were in a high forest of red cedar and Engelmann spruce when Stenson suddenly reined to a halt. "I want to talk," he said, not turning around. Fargo motioned for Jody to move up to the man's left side while he drew up on the right.

"I'm listening," Fargo said.

"This is as far as I go," Stenson said.

"That's not your call," Fargo answered.

"It's my neck," Stenson said.

"I told you I'll see that nothing happens to you," Jody said.

Stenson looked at her. "Can you guarantee that?" he asked.

Jody hesitated and saw Fargo nodding his head at her. She swallowed down the moment of hesitancy that had caught her up. "Yes," she said, trying to sound convincing and failing.

"That the best you can do, honey?" Stenson said, picking up on her tone.

"He'll listen to me," Jody said, trying to gather confidence within herself.

"What'll you say to him?" Stenson asked, leaning toward her, his voice anxious. He seemed to be asking for reassurance.

"I'll tell him not to change how I feel about him," Jody answered, the honesty in her voice very real.

"You really think he'll listen?" Stenson asked.

"I do," Jody said. Stenson let his shoulders drop in a little gesture of resignation. A split second later he exploded, diving from the saddle to slam into Jody. Fargo saw her fall from her horse with Stenson wrapped around her, cursing as he brought the Colt up. He pulled it back at once as Stenson disappeared with Jody below him. He had lulled them into a moment of relaxing. Cursing, Fargo leaped from the saddle and ran around the other two horses. He skidded to a halt as he saw Stenson with his arms wrapped around Jody's neck.

"I'll break her damn neck," the man threatened. "Back off!" Fargo halted, taking a step backward. "Throw your gun over here," Stenson ordered. Fargo hesitated, aware that he could be inviting a bullet. Yet he realized he had no choice. Stenson could end Jody's life with one twist of his arms and Fargo saw the desperation in the man's eyes. He saw something else, a fear that was consuming. Stenson was absolutely convinced of his fate if he fell into Bill Tillman's hands. The man's words, his actions, his desperation—they all added up to something more, messages he'd sort out later, Fargo promised himself. But now he had to make a choice, not that there was much choosing to be done.

Swearing under his breath, he tossed the Colt, seeing it land alongside Stenson. The man flung Jody aside as he seized the Colt, and rose to his feet. Backing away, his eyes locked on Fargo. Roy Stenson reached his horse and pulled himself into the saddle. He sent the horse into an instant gallop as he raced away. Thoughts leaped through Fargo's mind. Stenson could have fired a shot and killed him, or at least wounded him. But he hadn't. "Stay here," he said to Jody as he vaulted onto the Ovaro and sent the horse after Roy Stenson. He quickly caught sight of the man through the gray dawn light, the Ovaro closing ground, maneuvering through the trees with the muscled grace that made it so special. Stenson heard the hoofbeats, and glanced back and saw Fargo in the trees. But, Fargo saw, the man didn't raise the Colt and fire. Fargo felt the moment of satisfaction go through him. He sent the Ovaro through the trees, drawing abreast of Stenson, starting to move closer yet staying in the trees.

Stenson stopped glancing at him and concentrated on steering his roan through the heavy forest terrain. Fargo pulled his lariat from its lariat strap on the fork swell. Stenson's horse had slowed considerably as it maneuvered through the narrow spaces between the cedars and again, Fargo relied on the agility of the Ovaro's heavily muscled hindquarters. He swerved, cut through narrow spaces, and closed in on Stenson. Spotting a gap in the cedars, Fargo sent the lariat spinning through the air as Stenson still concentrated on maneuvering his horse. At the last moment, perhaps feeling a swish of air, Stenson turned in the saddle as the rope came down on him. He tried to twist away but the lariat caught him around his right arm. Fargo yanked the noose tight, pulled hard, and Roy Stenson flew from his horse.

Fargo leaped from the Ovaro as Stenson hit the ground, and started toward the man. Stenson half rose, pulled the lariat from his arm, and reached for the Colt. Fargo dived, landing on Stenson just as the man had the gun out of the holster, and drove his forearm into Stenson's throat. He heard the man's rush of breath as he gagged, his body growing limp for a moment. Fargo's arm swept out, his hand slamming into the Colt, sending the gun skittering out of Stenson's grip. Fargo rolled and started for the gun when he felt Stenson's arms around his throat, the power in the man's beefy form quickly apparent. Fargo felt his breath being cut off, so he dug his knees into the ground enough to give himself a few inches of room and flung himself sideways. Stenson went with him as he rolled, but the man's grip loosened and Fargo quickly drove an elbow into Stenson's belly. The man grunted, fell away, and Fargo rolled free. He started again for where the Colt lay on the ground, expecting Stenson would be going for the gun, too.

But as he reached the gun, he saw Stenson leaping onto his horse and racing away once more. Fargo clasped his hand around the Colt as Roy Stenson raced into the cedars, and raised the gun to fire. But he lowered it at once. He pushed to his feet, holstered the Colt and picked up the rifle where it had fallen as he returned to his horse. There was little to be gained by chasing after Roy Stenson, he reflected as he turned the Ovaro around and made his way back to Jody. He handed her the rifle as her eyes questioned him. "He's alive," Fargo said. "He got away. I kind of let him after I got my Colt back. I think he told me everything he had to say, maybe more than he realized."

"Such as?" Jody asked as she climbed onto her horse.

"That we're close to Bill Tillman's main camp."

"He told you that?"

"By not firing a shot at me. He knew we were close enough for a shot to be heard and bring others around, and he didn't want that," Fargo said.

"What else did he tell you without saying so?" Jody asked.

"That he's a man very afraid of tangling with your uncle," Fargo said.

"Anything else?"

"He's a man who wants to stay low, not run head-on into your uncle's problems. I'm thinking maybe he didn't have Jimmy Donovan gunned down. It doesn't fit with him," Fargo said.

"Then who did?"

Fargo shrugged. "Maybe there's somebody else who'd be happy if Bill Tillman disappeared, somebody who didn't want me finding him," he said. "Right now, let's see what's waiting for us up ahead." He sent the pinto forward along the high plateau, keeping the horse at a walk through the thick cedars. The sun had come out and sprinkled through the trees to make a carpet of dappled gold across the forest floor.

His eyes moved back and forth as they rode, ceaselessly scanning branches, leaves, brush, and forest grass, mostly nodding bromegrass, for any message he could read, much like other men read newspapers. A flash of blue caught his eye to the right and he followed it to where a high lake came into sight, filled with perhaps a thousand logs held behind a splash dam. He rode along the edge of the lake, found the spill gate, and then saw the river below, a few dozen logs resting against the bank. The river was calm, he saw, hardly moving, as if it waited for the moment when the logs would be sent cascading down from the high lake. Turning back into the forest but keeping the lake and the river below it still in sight, Fargo moved forward when he suddenly heard sounds and slowed the horse.

The sharp blows of axes came to his ears first, then voices that grew in strength and number as he and Jody drew closer. Reining to a halt, he dismounted, tethered the pinto to a low branch, and waited while Jody did the same with her horse. She was beside him as he moved forward on foot. They had gone another thousand or so yards when the trees thinned out enough for Fargo to see the cleared land and the three large cabins on it, the nearest one the largest. His brow furrowed as his eyes swept the site. Beyond the three cabins, a loose rope corral had been strung from the trees. Inside it, he saw some fifty or sixty horses. Alongside the rope corral, he saw men, some on their blankets, others standing in clusters, all with their saddles and gear on the ground beside them. He also saw four stacks of rifles nearby.

His eyes traveled across the camp again and noted a half-dozen loggers chopping wood while others were setting a row of logs into place, clearly meant for only one thing: a barricade. Jody pulled on his sleeve. "What's all this?" she whispered.

"Damned if I know," Fargo said. "Looks like a small army. The men with the horses are no loggers, that's for sure."

The door of the nearest cabin opened and a tall, well-built man stepped out. He halted outside the cabin, his eyes surveying the scene. Even before he heard Jody's sharp gasp, he knew the man, instantly recognizing the same straight figure, the same dusty blond hair, the same straight nose and high cheekbones. But mostly, the same commanding, opaque ice-fire blue eyes as Darlene's. He felt Jody move, excitement prodding her, and his hand clamped down on her arm. "No," he hissed. "Don't move a damn finger."

7

"It's Uncle Bill," she said.

"I know who it is," Fargo said with a hiss. "And it's not reunion time." She frowned at him as he nodded to the fifty or so men and horses. "I don't know what this is all about but your Uncle Bill may not be happy to see us," he said.

"Of course he'll be happy to see me," Jody said looking hurt that he should think otherwise.

"Probably, but we'll be finding out my way in my time," Fargo said sternly. She gave a pout.

"You've found him. Why wait?" she insisted.

He regarded her with impatience. "You still see him as a warm, benevolent figure? After everything you've seen and heard? You've that short a memory?" he pushed at her.

She pulled her lips tight. "There's nothing wrong with my memory," she said.

"You just like making excuses," he said.

"I like seeing the man I knew. I like thinking he's still there," she said.

"Thinking won't make it so," he said.

"It might. You think good of people and they live up to it," she said.

"Miss Naive," he said, but not harshly. "If you're right, you'll find out but only when I have my neck protected." He pulled at her as he started to crawl backward into the trees. He halted only when they were far enough back to be safe yet still allow him to see the campsite. As he watched, Bill Tillman moved through the site, paused to talk to the men by the horses, then went on to supervise setting up another line of log barricades. By the time the day drifted to an end, the barricades fronted the entire length of the campsite. Bill Tillman's tall, straight form continued to move through the site, supervising it, until the darkness descended.

A half-dozen cooking fires were lit and the men took turns bringing their food to be warmed on tin plates. Fargo stretched the stiffness out of his body as Jody leaned her head on his chest. "What's it all mean?" she asked, her voice troubled.

"Wish I knew. He's gathered a small army, certainly not for logging. He's getting ready for something.

"Maybe something we don't know about, an attack from someplace we've never heard about," Jody said.

"That doesn't explain his running off in the night, disappearing, not saying anything to his daughter. Why'd he do that?" Fargo said.

"Maybe he didn't want to worry her?" Jody suggested.

"That's putting a nice face on it." Fargo smiled and kissed her cheek. "You've a way of doing that. It's nice," he said. Her lips came to his at once, lingered, and then finally pulled back.

"You don't buy my explanation," she said, a hint of reproach in her voice.

"I don't buy anything, but I aim to find out," Fargo said, sitting up as the cooking fires began to burn out. When he rose, the camp was dark and still except for the restlessness of the horses. "Time to go calling," he said and pulled Jody up with him. He circled to the far edge of the camp before leaving the trees. He scanned the perimeters for sentries and found none. Going around the end of the barricades to the largest cabin, he saw candlelight flicker from the high window as he came to the outside wall. Raising himself on the balls of his feet, he could just peer over the edge of the window.

Bill Tillman sat at a battered desk, a half-empty bottle of whiskey at his elbow as he studied a large sheet of paper laid out before him. It seemed to be some sort of map. Tillman took a swallow from the bottle as Fargo lowered himself. Staying against the side of the cabin, he motioned for Jody to follow him. When he reached the door, he pressed himself against the cabin wall and let Jody go before him. "You're on, honey," he whispered. "Knock."

She gathered herself, straightened her back, her full breasts pushing out as she took a deep breath and rapped softly on the door. Bill Tillman opened in moments and Fargo heard the astonishment flood his voice. "My God," he gasped. "What in hell?"

"Hello, Uncle Bill," Jody said and rushed into his arms. He embraced her in a bear hug that lifted her from the ground.

"By God, what are you doing here, girl?" Tillman

asked and pulled her into the cabin. "How'd you get here?" he wondered, and started to shut the door when Fargo moved in quick, catlike steps that sent him into the cabin on Jody's heels. Bill Tillman stepped back, his brow furrowing, his ice blue eyes darkening. "What the hell is this?" he rasped.

"This is Fargo. I came with him, Uncle Bill," Jody said. The man's eyes bored into Fargo like cold diamond drills.

"You can stop running," Fargo said evenly.

The man's strong face remained still, as if carved in stone. "Didn't think you'd find me," he said, a grudging admission.

"Almost didn't," Fargo admitted.

Tillman turned to Jody. "What are you doing with him?" he asked icily.

"I ran away from Darlene. I was afraid to stay there. She kept me a prisoner," Jody said.

"I shouldn't have left you with her. Didn't figure on her taking it out on you," Tillman said and turned to Fargo. "Didn't figure her hiring you to find me, either."

"Why'd you run away and disappear? She's very concerned over you. She told me she was afraid something had happened to you," Fargo said.

Tillman's face broke into a grimace of a smile. "The concerned daughter. The goddamn timber-shaking worried daughter. Now, that's touching, real touching," he roared and Fargo's eyes narrowed on the man. "You know why I ran, Fargo. I ran because I was afraid somebody was going to kill me. And you know who that somebody was? Darlene, my darling daughter Darlene. How about that, mister?"

Fargo felt the surprise course through him, and casting a glance at Jody, he saw her own face wreathed in shock, her mouth hanging open. "It's hard to believe," Fargo said.

"Believe it. I guess I taught her too well," Tillman said.

"Why, Uncle Bill? What's all this about?" Jody broke in.

"It's about owning the thousands of acres that Tillman Logging owns. It's about controlling the richest timberland in the West," Tillman said.

"But you own Tillman Logging. I don't understand," Jody said.

Tillman's laugh was a bitter sound. "I thought I did," he said. "I took it, all prime logging land. It was mine, everybody knew that. Never filed any claims. Most folks didn't in those days. I just kept adding more pieces to what I had."

"Adding more pieces," Fargo echoed. "Is that a nice way of saying you took other people's land?"

"Everybody took land. That's the way it was done. I don't take any blame for that," Tillman said.

"Not everybody would agree with that," Fargo replied. "But you haven't really explained anything. Where does Darlene come into this?"

"The damn government came into it first," Tillman said, pounding a fist on the desk. "First they passed a bill that said all land holdings had to be formally filed with a land agent or they'd be up for anybody to claim. I took my time getting around to filing my claims. I was too busy running a logging operation. When I finally got around to it, I got myself a real big surprise. Claims for all of my land had been filed. By guess who?"

"Darlene," Jody breathed, awe filling her voice.

"Bull's-eye. Darlene, my own darling daughter who's so concerned over me now," Tillman bit out.

Fargo let the man's story run through his mind again. "I can understand how angry you'd be at that, but I don't see how it means that Darlene wants to kill you. You're sure you're not letting your imagination run away with you?" he questioned.

"I'm goddamn sure!" Tillman shouted.

"Look, she's filed the claims. She's got the land. What more does she need? Seems to me she's got it all under control," Fargo pointed out.

"You don't know the rest of it," Tillman countered. "The government came into it again. They passed the Land Auction Act. It said that any land without a proper, registered claim was homestead or squatter land, and could be sold at auction. It didn't make any difference to Washington how long a family had the land or how many lifetimes they'd worked it. It could be put up for auction to the highest bidder."

"But that act wouldn't affect Darlene. She had already registered the claims," Fargo said.

"That's right, and I was out, stripped of everything. Or so she thought. She laughed at me, told me I could stay on as a windfall bucker or a spar man. I figured I was finished, everything lost to that little scheming bitch I'd raised. That's just what she thought, too. But then the government came into it again. The Land Auction Act was so unfair, stripping so many people of the land they'd worked for a lifetime, that land agents were being shot right and left. Washington rushed to pass the Preemption Act."

"What'd that do?" Fargo asked and saw Tillman's blue eyes take on a new fiery light as a tight smile edged his lips.

"It said that the people they'd called homesteaders and squatters could buy their land for a dollar twenty-five an acre. All they had to do was show that they had lived on the land or worked it for two years or more and they could buy it instead of having it put up for auction." Tillman let out a roar of triumphant laughter. "Suddenly all of Darlene's claims didn't mean shit. The Preemptive Act gave me the right to buy all my land for a dollar and a quarter an acre. I'd damned well lived and worked on the land, so I came under the provisions of the act. She didn't have a damn thing except claims that were useless to her. I put down a cash payment to the government that secured the land for me as a homesteader."

Fargo's lips pursed as Tillman's story sank into him. "I can see why that made her real angry," he commented.

"She went crazy, screamed, made all kinds of threats, told me I'd never live to finish buying it all back. I laughed at her, shrugged off everything she threatened to do, until I got word that she meant every word of what she said. We kept fighting, she and I, but I knew there was more behind her words now. Word came to me she was trying to contact two gunslingers."

"Word that came through Dolly at the saloon?" Fargo put in.

"That's unimportant," Tillman said.

"That's when you decided to run and disappear in the night," Fargo said.

"Didn't fancy being murdered in my bed," Tillman said. "She's cold enough to do anything. I cut out, stayed low. That's when I heard she was looking to hire you to find me."

Fargo felt his eyes narrowing at the man, the dark thought springing up inside him taking on grim shape. "You didn't want that," he said.

"Of course not," Tillman said.

"It was your men who killed Jimmy Donovan," Fargo said, venom coating his words. Tillman's shrug was a soulless admission. "You had a poor, innocent kid gunned down so he wouldn't deliver a message," Fargo said.

"If he didn't find you, you'd be on your way and long gone," Tillman said. "I sent my boys to track him down before he got to you."

"Oh, my. Oh, my," Fargo heard Jody's voice gasp.

"You bastard," Fargo said.

Tillman shrugged again. "Sentiment is a dangerous indulgence," he said, his ice-fire blue eyes meeting Fargo's fury. "Say it, whatever your thinking," he urged.

"I'm thinking the apple doesn't fall far from the tree. Like father, like daughter," Fargo said. "Both of you will do anything to get what you want."

"Family trait, I guess. Only I'm going to win," the man said. "But that's not your problem. Your problem is that you found me. That's unfortunate, for you."

"Hell it is. I'm walking out of here and I'm taking Jody with me," Fargo said.

"I'm afraid you won't be doing either. Jody came with you to be with me. She's staying," Tillman said. Fargo drew his Colt, feeling uneasiness sweep through him as the man smiled. Men didn't smile when he drew a Colt on them.

"Let's go, Jody," Fargo said.

"You stay right there, Jody," Tillman ordered sternly.

Fargo's eyes went to Jody and saw the shock still clinging to her face, but now consternation and indecision joined the emotions that seized her. She turned to Bill Tillman. "There has to be some way you and Darlene can work this out, Uncle Bill," she tried.

"It's past working out. I raised a damn serpent. Now, I've got to crush it," Tillman said. "It's the only way. She won't back off. You know that."

"Maybe I could talk to her, try to convince her to. Or maybe Fargo could," Jody said. She was desperately trying to find some way out, Fargo knew. But he knew there was none. Bill Tillman wasn't any more interested than Darlene was interested. It was a family feud, the kind that invoked a hatred and bitterness far deeper than any between ordinary rivals. It was always that way when families fought, the wounds deeper, more personal, with roots of hurt and ingratitude, of expectations shattered, with only unreachable bitterness remaining.

"Let's go, Jody," he said quietly, seeing the despair in her eyes. She started toward him but her gaze remained on Tillman.

"I'm sorry, Uncle Bill," she said. "I feel like I don't know you anymore, putting men in flumes, gunning down that young messenger. I've seen too much and heard even more. I've got to think about all of it, work it out inside myself."

She started past him. When she reached Fargo, Tillman's voice followed. "You're staying here, girl. We'll talk about it, just you and I, the way we always did. There are things you don't understand, that you don't realize. You have to learn about them. I'll help you, as always."

Jody shook her head, her quiet stubbornness asserting itself as she halted beside Fargo. "No, I have to think this all out by myself," she said quietly. She came with Fargo as he opened the door. He stepped out and halted, facing the six rifles aimed at him from a half circle.

"Shit," he muttered softly. He eyed the array of firepower, and saw it was too much and too close to take on. Besides, the hail of bullets would almost certainly find Jody. He lowered the Colt as Tillman stepped from the cabin, his smile deprecating.

"You didn't see any sentries. You thought that was overconfidence," the man said and Fargo cursed silently. "Three of my men stay behind the far cabin on the hill. Their orders are to keep their eyes on my cabin as soon as night falls. They saw you arrive, called in the others, and came down," Tillman said, reaching over and taking the Colt from Fargo's hand. Fargo cursed silently again. He had underestimated the man's cleverness and he should have realized Tillman would have sentries somewhere.

"My mistake," he muttered.

"We pay for our mistakes," Tillman said. "I heard that you escaped from the flume. Nobody's ever done that. I'm really impressed. You're going to get another chance in a day or two."

"No!" Jody's word tore from her. "You can't do that, Uncle Bill."

"This is none of your business, Jody. Stay out of it," Tillman said severely.

"Let him go and I'll stay with you," Jody said.

Tillman gave her another of his deprecatory smiles. "You're staying anyway, my dear," he said. "You'll be comfortable and I'll see that you're safe." He gestured to the guards. "Take him to the last cabin. Keep two men in front of the door at all times," he said. Three of the guards stepped forward, one on each side of him, the third at his back. They started to march him off when Jody leaped forward and wrapped her arms around him.

"I'm sorry, I'm sorry," she murmured. He held her for a moment.

"Not your fault, none of it," he said, and pressed his lips to the top of her head before another of the guards pulled her away.

"Seems you've filled little Jody's head with a lot of wrong ideas," Tillman said as the guards led Fargo away. "I'll fix that."

"Like hell," Fargo flung back. "You won't change what she's seen and learned. Your excuses won't make that go away."

Tillman's lips twitched in an attack of barely controlled fury. "I'm going to personally watch them put you back in the flume," he said.

"Good. You can watch me escape a second time," Fargo tossed back at Tillman as the guards pushed him forward. It was a gesture of defiance, he knew. Nothing more. Without the knife that had given him a grip to fling himself over the edge of the flume, he didn't have a chance to escape. He let the grimness of the situation sweep over him as the three men led him to the last cabin, which was considerably smaller than the others. They pushed him inside, where he saw a candle burning, thick and squat, and a single cot under one high window. The door slammed shut behind him and as he listened, he heard the two guards taking up positions on the other side of the door.

He frowned up at the small, high window and wondered why they had left him in a room with a window while they stayed outside the door. He went to the cot, stood up on it to where he could reach the window, and found his question answered. On the other side of the window, invisible from the floor of the room in the night, rows of barbed wire were strung in a crisscross pattern. He stared at the wire, a sawtooth variety he had never seen before, but plainly able to cut a hand to ribbons.

He dropped down on the cot, sat back against the wall, and was able to glimpse up at the sky by looking out through the window. The moon was curving its way downward. It would reach the horizon in a few hours, he guessed, and dawn would quickly follow. Tillman was still involved with protecting the site. He'd probably wait another day before taking his prisoner to the flume, Fargo surmised. The small army of men and horses had to mean that Bill Tillman expected trouble. He expected Darlene would eventually find him through one means or another, and he was preparing for that moment. Fargo found his thoughts leapfrogging to Darlene. She had been careful and clever. She'd presented only the face of a concerned daughter, but it was plain now that her frigid blue eyes were but a reflection of the two people in one that she was. He found himself wondering about the night she'd made love to him.

Had it been one more way to encourage him to search for her father? Or had it been one side of her double self, her fiery side that often reflected in her eyes? His thoughts stayed on Darlene Tillman. He wanted to get to her. He'd earned his hire—he'd found Bill Tillman. He wanted to tell her, out of principle, or perhaps he was simply angry enough to tell her what he'd learned. She had lied to him from the very beginning. She'd been a lot more than a concerned daughter. She no doubt realized that if he knew what she was all about, he would have never taken the job.

His lips tightened as he swore to himself. It was all idle conjecture unless he could find a way out of the cabin, and that was growing less likely with every passing hour. Day would make it impossible, he knew as he rose, going over to the door and putting his ear against it. The two guards were having a monosyllabic exchange, both very much awake. He returned to the cot and stretched out and knew the feeling of helplessness as time continued to slide away. He estimated there was perhaps another hour of darkness left and he rose, stood on the cot again, and peered at the barbed wire. There was no way he could pull it loose, not without thick leather gloves or a heavy metal-cutting shears, and he lowered himself dejectedly back on the cot. Not more than a few minutes had passed when a sound interrupted the silence—stones were being tossed into the window.

Swinging his long legs around, Fargo jumped up onto the cot and peered out through the barbed wire. Jody was there below the window and she waved when she saw his face. She held her arm up and he saw the coil of a lariat. Standing back a few paces, she tossed the rope at the window and it hit, catching against the edges of the barbed wire and hanging there. Reaching out carefully, avoiding the deadly barbs, he pulled the rope in, then began to wrap it around a strand of the wire. When he had it wrapped tightly, he used his feet as leverage against the wall, and bringing all the strength of his powerful shoulder and arm muscles into play, he pulled, felt the strand of wire give, bend, then come loose, and finally tear out of the wooden windowsill to which it was attached.

He pulled the barbed strand into the room, unwrapped the rope, and began to wind it around the next strand. He braced himself again, pulled hard, and the metal wire strand came loose, more easily this time. Working silently, he finally had all the barbed wire strands pulled from the window. Fargo coiled up the lariat and pushed it from the window to the ground. He secured one end of it to the leg of the cot, making sure the leg was wedged tight into the corner of the room, and climbed from the window. Lowering himself down the rope, he felt his feet touch ground and in seconds Jody was against him, clutching him tightly to her. Motioning for her to be silent, he edged his way along the back of the cabin, and chanced a quick glance around the corner.

One of the two guards wasn't more than a dozen feet from him, he saw. The second man lounged a few yards beyond. Fargo tensed every muscle. He'd have to strike with the speed of a rattler, taking out both men almost simultaneously. Drawing a deep breath, he whirled around the corner of the cabin, and was at the nearest man in two long strides. The man began to turn as Fargo's sweeping right uppercut crashed into his jaw. He went down, Fargo scooping his rifle up before it hit the ground. The second guard, his senses kicking in, spun around just in time to take the butt of the rifle that Fargo slammed straight into his throat. His eyes popped out, his hands clawed at his throat for an instant, and then he pitched forward and lay still.

They'd both be unconscious as the dawn rose, Fargo thought in satisfaction. Yanking the door open, he went inside and pulled the lariat back through the window, undid it from the leg of the cot, and had it coiled again as he went back outside to find Jody. She clung to him, her body hot but not trembling this time. "How'd you manage it?" he asked.

"I promised him I wouldn't run away. He left me

alone in the cabin without any guards. He knows I keep my word," Jody said.

"He was wrong this time," Fargo said.

"No. I just didn't promise I wouldn't try to help you escape," she said. "I circled back to the Ovaro and got your lariat."

"Which I'm taking. That way there's nothing to tie you into being here tonight. They'll figure I somehow worked my way out," Fargo said.

"What are you going to do?" Jody asked.

"Go back to Darlene. Tell her I found him and where. I keep my word, too," he said.

Jody's little smile was wry. "I guessed as much," she said.

"Then I'm coming back here for you," he said. "Until then, play along with him. Be the sweet, hero-worshipping little niece he knew. Don't antagonize him. He's a ruthless bastard." He saw the sadness cloud over her face, the terrible regret of the disillusioned, as she nodded. "Truth can hurt," he said gently. "There's a limit to looking away."

She lifted her head and her lips pressed his, a bittersweet kiss before she stepped back. "Hurry. Get away from here," she said and she turned and broke into a run as he crouched. He saw the first faint streaks of dawn touch the sky as he reached the Ovaro and realized he hadn't his Colt. He thought for a moment of going back to try and get it, but soon realized it was a suicidal thought. He sent the Ovaro into a fast trot and hurried through the cedars, wanting to put plenty of distance between himself and the camp as the sun touched the sky.

around to look toward the tree. His hands were fully
six inches above the roofline of the corrals. "Don't
let your men forget to fire the door," Bill Tillman
said to one of the men. He turned and looked at the
tree closed. As Fargo rode at the cabin low creek

8

Fargo retraced his steps, and the sun was already
high when he passed the flume. He slowed and
turned the horse to stop at the edge of the V-shaped
device. His eyes scanned the smooth inner sides of
the chute until he finally found where he had thrust
in the knife, its blade still imbedded in the wood.
But the hilt of the knife was gone, snapped off, and
ground to bits. He peered at the blade, saw that it
was too deeply imbedded to pry loose without
tools, and so he rode on. Another hour brought him
to a spot where he heard the sound of bucksaws and
axes and he made a wide circle around them as he
went on his way. Tillman had plainly left orders for
logging operations to go on as usual. A clever move,
Fargo conceded. It kept everything looking normal.

Fargo didn't push the Ovaro, the thick forest terrain hard on even a perfectly muscled, conditioned
animal. He spotted the lake after almost the entire
day had gone and the buildings of the main Tillman
compound came into sight. He rode toward the
main house with its impressive stone and log fa-
cade. Beyond it, as the bunkhouses and corrals
stretched out, his eyes scanned the scene, the furrow

digging into his brow. At least fifty horses were tethered on long ropes or roaming in the corrals. Small knots of men lounged near the trees. Bill Tillman wasn't the only one who had amassed a small army of gunfighters. As Fargo rode to the main house and dismounted, a tall, lean figure hurried outside in the last slanting rays of sun, her dusty blond hair glinting, the white, tailored shirt following the curve of her breasts.

Darlene came to him, her callous, frosty eyes searching his face. "I'd given you up," she said. "I was sure something had happened to you."

"Plenty happened to me," Fargo said grimly. "Were you pacing the floor with worry?"

Her eyes narrowed. "Something like that," she said.

His eyes went to the men and horses by the bunkhouses. "You've been busy," he commented.

"I had to be. I decided maybe you weren't coming back. I got ready to search for myself. I knew I'd need a lot of help," Darlene said and then led him into the house, taking his arm with firm possessiveness. Fargo threw another glance at the men and horses. Her answer was just one more lie, of course, he thought. She had been preparing her small army for an all-out assault on Bill Tillman from the very beginning. She had hired him just to pinpoint her target. Inside the house, her arms slid around his neck. "I'm glad you're back, Fargo. I hope you're going to tell me what I want to hear." Her mouth found his, and he had no trouble remembering the hot fervency of her passion. But she pulled back after a moment. "What's the matter?" she asked. "You forget so soon?"

"It's not about forgetting. It's about learning," he said.

"Meaning what?"

"You left a lot out," Fargo said calmly.

Her wintry blue eyes narrowed again. "That sounds like you found him," she said carefully.

"Doesn't it?" he said.

"Don't play games with me," she said, frost forming instantly on each word.

"Fair play. You played games with me," he said. "You didn't send me to find someone you were worried over. You sent me to find someone you intend killing."

"I hired you to do a job. You took the money."

"That's right," he said. "That's the only reason why I came back."

"Whatever," she said coldly. "Where is he?"

"Up north. A big logging camp," Fargo said and felt the sourness in his mouth, though not from any concern for Tillman or for Darlene. A conscience can bring its own bitterness, he reflected. He watched the slow smile spread across Darlene's face.

"I know the place," she said. "It'll take till morning to get there. I'll start right now."

"No. I want time to get back there first," Fargo said.

"Why?" she frowned.

"Jody is with him. I want to get her out of there before you go charging in," Fargo said.

"I don't give a goddamn about Jody. I'm not waiting," Darlene snapped.

"I want to go back, first," Fargo demanded again.

"You stay here. You going back might set off an alarm with him. Right now he's playing his big uncle role with Jody, as he always did. That's the way I want it. I'll give him a surprise party the likes of which he's never had," Darlene said.

Fargo considered telling her that Tillman had his own surprise party waiting for her but he pulled back from the thought. He'd come back and kept his agreement. He had no cause to do more, no reason to interfere in their orgy of killing and deception, no need to help either side. He'd let them destroy each other and applaud. The world would be a better place without either of them.

"Maybe you're right. Maybe I ought to just stay here," he told Darlene.

"Of course," she said. "Use the guest room. Get a good rest. I'll show you how grateful I can be when I get back." She turned and strode from the room and Fargo went into the guest room. He lit a candle as darkness fell, and then peered from the window. He saw the commotion as horses were saddled, riders moving from the corrals. He picked out Darlene. She'd changed from the white, tailored shirt to a dark red one and was leading her small army out of the compound. He turned away, and stretched out on the bed.

He'd give them time to get a good start. They'd be moving slowly through the dense forest terrain, especially at night. Even by day, there were too many of them to make time through the forests. He let himself doze, absorbing the restoring powers of sleep, even in small doses. Finally he awoke again, and swung from the bed to go into the kitchen, where he found some cold chicken legs that were more than enough to assuage his appetite. He left the house, and was striding toward the Ovaro when two shots exploded. One whistled past his ear, the other hit a fencepost only inches from him. He dove, hit the ground, and rolled as three more shots exploded into the earth around his feet. There were two shooters, he realized as he rolled again, coming up against the flagstones in front of the house.

Another volley of bullets resounded, at least three hitting the flagstones. But now he was running, bent over in a crouch. He hit the front door of the house with his shoulder and it flew open as he went sprawling inside, kicking the door shut just as two more bullets thudded into it. He rose and retreated from the door. They'd come bursting in spewing bullets any second, he was certain, so he retreated to the kitchen and looked around for something he could use as a weapon. He spotted a small cleaver, and scooping it up, saw a side door from the kitchen, and stepped to the edge of it. He cursed Darlene's cleverness as he waited. She hadn't taken any chances, leaving the two shooters to wait in case he tried to leave, which was just what he'd done.

It took but a few seconds more for the front door to burst open and the two men rushed in, both sending a barrage of bullets ahead of them. They emptied their guns, halting to reload as they saw only an empty living room in front of them. Fargo was reluctant to get rid of his only weapon but the two men were almost finished reloading. He drew back the arm holding the cleaver, realizing it felt very much like a tomahawk in his hand. He took aim and let the cleaver sail through the air, smashing the nearest figure on the side of his head.

The man cried out as a torrent of red spouted from his head, staggering sideways as the gun fell from his hand. He collapsed with the cleaver still imbedded just in front of his ear. Fargo saw the second man recover from his surprise, half turn, and fire a volley of shots at the kitchen doorway. They all slammed harmlessly into the wall behind Fargo as he ran from the kitchen and out into the hallway. He heard the man's footsteps chasing after him as he ran into the guest room and picked up the candle. Pressing himself at the edge of the doorway, he waited, not breathing, and watched the man's shadow approach the doorway. The man's gun hand came into sight, held out before him as he cautiously advanced through the doorway. Fargo whirled, and plunged the candle into the man's hand. "Owoooo, Jesus!" the man screamed as the gun fell from his fingers. Fargo's left fist whistled in a short arc, and caught the man on the point of the jaw. He flew backward into the living room and went down.

Fargo followed, bent low to smash another blow, and had to twist away as the man kicked up out at him. He came forward again but the man scuttled backward, regained his feet, and Fargo had a chance to see unkempt hair over a rawboned face and eyes that were mean but not strong. The man aimed a left at him followed with a right, and Fargo parried both blows. He shot a quick left jab out that sent the man's head back. He followed with another quick jab and again the man's head snapped back, his messy hair flying up from his head. As Fargo came in again, the man danced away, circling around to avoid backing into the sofa.

Suddenly, the man swerved, diving toward a small writing table against one wall of the room. Frowning, Fargo started after him when he saw the man pick up a letter opener from the table, a long-bladed, sharp instrument with a horn handle. Not quite a knife, yet it would do just as well plunged into a man's chest, Fargo saw. Emboldened by his new weapon, the man came forward and slashed out as Fargo ducked away, the weapon cutting the air above his head. He retreated as the man pressed on, slashing again with the letter opener, this time trying to drive the weapon straight forward. Fargo sucked his abdomen in as the weapon whistled within inches of him. He backed away again as his foe rushed forward, holding the weapon out in front of him, ready to try another lunge. Fargo set himself, rising up on the balls of his feet. He was ready as the man lurched forward to drive the letter-opener into his stomach. Again, Fargo sucked himself in as the blade neared his stomach. But this time he brought a crashing blow down on the man's wrist. "Jesus!" the man cried out in pain as the weapon dropped from his grip and he bent forward to grab his injured wrist.

Fargo's left cross landed on the point of his jaw, his right following instantly, and the man launched backward, his head hitting the side of a heavy wood lounging chair. He fell sprawling and lay still. Fargo straightened, turned, and strode past him into the kitchen, picking up the six-gun, a Remington-Beals six-shot single-action army revolver, and pushed it into his holster. It would have to do until he could retrieve his Colt. He left the house at a trot, swung onto the Ovaro, and sent the horse through the night.

He set a steady pace. Without pushing the Ovaro, he'd still easily catch up to the fifty riders finding their way through the dense forests. Fargo retraced steps with the signs and marks already imprinted inside him from his previous trips, a practice that had long ago become automatic. Peering through the thick leaves overhead from time to time, he saw the moon had crossed the midnight sky just as his ears picked up the sounds of men and horses in front of him. He let a snort bordering on contempt escape his lips. Fifty Sioux or Cheyenne, to say nothing of Comanche, could negotiate a thick forest almost noiselessly. But not these ragtag riders. He veered to one side, executing a wide circle around them as he went forward. He passed the bulk of them and tried to catch a glimpse of Darlene. But the darkness and the forest refused him that as he rode on. When he had outdistanced them, he slowed to let the Ovaro rest some, and finally he found himself moving up the long slope and onto the high plateau.

The trees thinned and his eyes swept the sky, seeing that the moon had disappeared down the horizon. Dawn would follow all too quickly, so he put the horse into a trot. The very first gray-pink streaks of the new day began to paint their way across the sky when he reached Bill Tillman's main logging camp. Fargo slowed as he moved toward the still-sleeping site. The horses were blowing and striking their hooves into the dirt as they felt the new day breaking. Fargo dismounted and proceeded to lead the Ovaro in a wide circle around the three main cabins as the dawn's light outlined each building. Was Jody still in the last cabin, he wondered, or had Tillman brought her down to the large cabin with him? He had to be especially careful, he knew. It was not a time for making mistakes. Rather, it was a time when all hell waited in the wings to break loose.

He indulged himself in hoping he could have Jody and himself away from here before that happened, and decided his first move was to secure the Ovaro into a cluster of cedars at the edge of the campsite. Tethering his horse out of sight, he moved into the open in a crouch, swearing softly as he saw the camp waking as the new day rushed to announce itself. The men were rising, stretching, and starting to tend to their hoses as Fargo sank to one knee beside a cluster of high serviceberry. He swept the camp again, his eyes going to the river and the hundred or so logs wedged against the shore, then moved his glance up to the high lake and the thousands of logs piled high behind the splash dam. He returned his eyes to the scene in front of them. Everyone was busy waking, doing morning chores such as seeing to their bedrolls and tending to their horses. Time was running out for him. He left the serviceberry, ran in a crouch to the rear of the last cabin, and threw himself to the ground when a man carrying a rifle moved into sight at the front of the cabin.

Crawling forward, Fargo reached the back of the cabin and knew the guard had given him the answer to his question. Jody was in this cabin. But under guard. Why, he wondered. Time was still running, activity growing stronger in the camp. He had to exchange boldness for caution before time would deprive him of both. Rounding the front of the cabin, he sprang forward, the six-gun in hand. The guard started to turn as Fargo brought the butt of the heavy Remington down on his head. He had just hit the ground unconscious when Fargo opened the cabin door and rushed inside. Jody sat up on a cot, the fright in her eyes quickly vanishing into welcome as she recognized the figure in the doorway.

She leaped up, her short nightgown flying up over her thighs as she flew into his arms. "Oh, God, oh, my God, you're alive!" she said, clinging to him.

"Get dressed," he said. "We're getting out of here." He watched her pull off the nightgown and wash herself with the water from a big, tin basin, and enjoyed the loveliness of her every motion. She pulled on clothes, and took a small traveling sack. "You might have to leave that," he said, holding her as she came to him. "Are you all right?" he asked, noting some consternation on her face. She nodded. "No problems with my escape?" he pressed.

"None that found their way into words," she said.

"But they found their way into a guard," he said and she nodded again.

"He said it was for my protection. He couldn't

vouch for all the gunhands he'd brought in," Jody said. "But I think he didn't completely believe you'd gotten out all on your own." He went to the door and peered out, seeing Bill Tillman's tall, straight figure with some of his gunhands. "How do you expect to get out without being caught? It's impossible. The place is crawling with people."

"I'd hoped I could get you out before everybody woke up but it's too late for that. We'll have to make a run for it while they're all fighting with each other," he said and Jody frowned back. "Darlene's going to arrive, any damn minute now. She's bringing her own little army. There's going to be one hell of a battle. That's going to be our cover." She took in his words but he saw the reservation in her eyes. He didn't blame her. He wasn't at all sure they could pull it off. But then, there wasn't another choice.

A sudden shout cut into his thoughts, the sound instantly ballooning into more hollers, the sound of feet running, and of horses being saddled. "She's here," Fargo said. "They heard her coming." He led Jody from the cabin, and instantly ran for the cover of a cluster of serviceberry. The camp had exploded into men running on foot, some on horseback, others manning the log barricades that had been erected. Fargo saw Bill Tillman directing the action, acting very much like a general. The next explosion of noise came from the trees that fronted the camp. Fargo saw a massed phalanx of riders burst from the trees, racing forward in irregular lines that quickly dissolved into small clusters of men choosing their own targets. He saw Tillman's men surge forward on foot and on horseback while others fought from behind the barricades.

Gunsmoke rose, thickening the air around them. "Let's go," Fargo said, pulling Jody up as he ran toward the trees at the left side of the logging camp, the river only a dozen yards beyond. Crouching as they ran, Fargo saw bullets plowing into the dirt at their feet, and heard shots hurtling over their heads. "They're not aiming at us," Jody said.

"No but a bullet's a bullet aimed or not," he said. "Keep low." He ran for a long ditch, and flung himself and Jody into it, then raised his head to peer out at the battle. The casualties were running high on both sides, he saw, with men going down fast and furiously. He tried to see Tillman but couldn't find him amidst the fight, and scanning the distance for Darlene, he failed to spot her, also.

Staying in the ditch, he moved forward, Jody behind him, following the ditch as it moved into the midst of the pitched battle and then turned toward the river. He stayed with it as it swung away from the very center of the battle and he paused, daring to lift his head and peer out. The ground was littered with bodies, some hanging over the barricades, most lying on the grass in the awkwardly arrested positions of violent and sudden death. The staccato roar of gunfire had lessened—dead men can't shoot. The pockets of shooting were now coming mostly from the tree line at the front of the camp. He wanted to circle around to where he'd hidden the Ovaro, but he discarded the plan. They'd be too big a target on horseback. Their best move was to somehow reach the forest and lay low there until it was over. But a sudden fusillade of gunfire told him that wouldn't be easy to do, either.

He halted where the ditch turned toward the river and began to come to an end. Another sweeping glance across the camp showed more bodies littering the ground. The battle seemed to be ending in a standoff between the few left alive. Again, he searched the grounds for Tillman or Darlene, and once again he saw neither. Suddenly, he heard Jody's gasp. "Fargo . . . oh, God, look," she said and he followed her gaze as she stared toward the river. Two figures were on the logs that stretched from the bank a few dozen yards into the calm water of the river. One was Tillman, the other Darlene. Each held a seven-foot long pole with a vicious hooked spike at the end, which loggers used to handle logs in the water. They faced each other, lunging at one another with the vicious, deadly poles.

Tillman was the taller and the stronger of the two, and he used his muscle to thrust and swipe with vicious strokes. But Darlene was quicker, her movements were fluid, and as Fargo watched with a combination of awe and fascination, he saw her avoid one of Tillman's lunges, parry his jab, and bring her own pole around in a quick upward swipe. Tillman's shoulder spurted blood where the hooked spike slashed it open. He roared in fury as he lunged again, and once more Darlene nimbly avoided the attack, bringing her pole downward in a fast chopping motion. Fargo saw Tillman's thigh tear open. Darlene grew overconfident, and rushed in for another slash when Tillman spun and slammed the back half of his pole into Darlene's ribs with all his strength. She flew a half-dozen feet, fell, and then scrambled to regain her footing on the logs when Tillman's pointed hook slashed a line across her back.

Her red shirt tore open, darkening as blood poured from her back. But she spun away, returning to face Tillman with her pole raised to strike. Fargo's eyes held on her patrician face for a moment, seeing the insane fury in her icy stare. He brought his gaze to Tillman's face and saw the mirror image of hatred gone berserk. But perhaps it had always been so, Fargo reflected, insanity brought to a terrible end by forces too deep to know, the seed gone feral from its own wildness. He saw Jody's eyes on him, horror and despair in their depths. "Family fun, Tillman style," he said. She looked away but not before glaring an angry reproach at him.

His own eyes narrowed at the two figures on the logs. One of them would win, and that was wrong. Neither deserved victory. Neither deserved to inflict their murderous ruthlessness on the world, and that would still happen, regardless of which of them won. It was a mockery of everything good, of truth and justice. Neither deserved to go on to perpetuate their evil designs. The gunfire, though less of it now, still rang out in the forest at the edge of the camp. Men were fighting to kill each other out of fear or defensiveness. And it was all an echo of the two figures battling on the logs in an insane struggle to let their ruthlessness triumph.

Wrong, all wrong, Fargo thought, and his hand closed on Jody's shoulder. "Stay here," he said.

"Where are you going?" she asked, alarm instant in her face.

"To fix things. Stop the world, maybe make it a better place. I'm not sure, only that I have to try," he said as he jumped from the ditch, and began to run for the edge of the forest. His eyes went to the high lake not more than a few thousand yards away where thousands of logs were piled up. He plunged into the trees, dropping down as a figure rose, a rifle in hand, firing at him. The man didn't know him. He only knew he wasn't on his side. Fargo rolled, came up on his stomach with the Remington in hand and fired as the rifleman tried to draw a bead on him. The man fell onto his face and lay still.

Fargo rose, and started to plunge through the trees again when two more figures appeared, bringing their guns up to fire. Flinging himself sideways, Fargo landed behind the trunk of a thick cedar as he heard the bullets slam into the tree. Once again, Fargo realized he was a fair target for both sides. He moved around to the far side of the tree, letting the two men come into sight as they started around the tree after him. His two shots brought them down as if they were attached to each other, both spinning and collapsing together.

Fargo ran again toward the high lake looming up in front him when two more figures crashed through the trees, both men carrying carbines. They saw him, surprise on their faces, and started to raise their weapons when Fargo fired. The nearest one toppled first, the other one managing a half-dozen steps before he fell. Once again, Fargo started forward when a figure dropped onto him from a low branch. He went down, dizzy from the impact, and knew he was on both knees while trying to shake his head clear. Dimly, he saw the kick coming at him, and he tried to turn away but the kick landed flush against his head. Fargo felt himself fall and roll, dimly hearing the footsteps coming after him. He tried to raise his gun and realized his hand was empty.

Shaking his head, he cleared his vision enough to see the man picking the Remington up from the ground. Fargo dove, hearing his own voice raised in a roar of fury. He hit the man at the knees and felt the bullet whistle over his head. The man went down, brought the pistol around, and fired again. But this time, the only sound was the dry click of the hammer on an empty chamber. Fargo drove his knee into the man's abdomen and the figure gasped and rolled away. Fargo clamped down on the revolver, yanked it from the man's hand, and slammed the barrel against the man's temple. The figure went limp, and lay on his side as Fargo pushed to his feet.

He ran forward again. He was almost at the high lake, the splash dam in front of him. His eyes went to the river below and the two figures on the logs. Tillman and Darlene were still fighting, lunging with their hooked poles, both covered in blood, their clothes shredded, Darlene's long breasts swinging as she lunged with her pole. He saw Tillman drop to one knee but his pole stayed raised. He was not finished yet, only finding strength for another moment, another chance for that final victory. Darlene was the Goddess of Hate, determined to have her triumph, something out of an evil nether world, waiting for her moment to conquer.

Fargo roared in rage as he leaped forward, racing to the gate of the splash dam. Heavy rope knots held it closed and he tore at them, yanking and pulling and straining until they opened. He leaped backward as the mountain of logs spilled from the lake, hurtling downward to the river with a tremendous rubbing, howling, roaring sound. They were traveling at a furious speed as they slammed into the water of the river below. Fargo saw Tillman and Darlene turn to look up, terror sweeping the fury from their faces. The cascade of logs smashed into the relatively few logs in the river and Fargo saw both Tillman and Darlene flung high into the air as the logs they stood on were upended and sent spiraling upward. Their figures disappeared in the gargantuan torrent of logs that rose and fell, sweeping forward, spilling over each other, and obliterating everything in their path.

Fargo dropped to one knee and felt the breath drain from him as below, the mass of logs, many still atop one another, began to move downriver. Rising to his feet, he started back through the cedars, suddenly aware of the eerie silence that had taken over the land. He made his way back down to the edge of the camp, and his eyes swept the still bodies that littered the ground with an expression that mixed anger and sorrow, bitterness, and incomprehension. He saw Jody stand up, step from the ditch, and come toward him. His eyes went to the logs that moved down the river as she leaned against him.

"One of them would have won," he said. "Were you willing to back either? Were you willing to choose sides?"

"No," she said after a moment. "Neither of them would have brought anything except more harm, more brutality, more ruthlessness to the world.

"Neither deserved to win," he said.

She took his hand as he walked to where he had left the Ovaro and then to Tillman's cabin, where he retrieved his Colt. She waited outside, refusing to go in. They found Jody's horse among dozens of others wandering into the forests on their own, and mounting it, she rode beside him as they set a leisurely pace into the forests. He turned, rode to the river, and let the horses wet their feet along the bank. The logs had swept downriver out of sight and the riverbank held a peaceful quietness. "What will happen to the Tillman land now?" Jody asked.

"It might be put up for auction under the Land Auction Act. Or maybe someone else will register a claim for it," Fargo said.

"Such as Roy Stenson?" Jody queried.

"I'd expect he'd put in a bid," Fargo said. "He'd finally stop being afraid. Living under a shadow can shrivel a man." Fargo rode on beside the river as the day began to fade and when he spied a luscious, heavy stand of peach leaf willow and rode to a halt under the dark green, narrow leaves. A thick bed of fern moss formed a soft carpet that ran all along the line of willows. "We'll bed down here," he said.

"Yes, this is a nice place, soft and quiet," she said.

The day ended and the night stayed warm and a full moon rose to bathe the willows in its pale light.

Jody came to him, slowly pulling off her clothes and giving him an eyeful of naked loveliness. "Make me forget everything that's happened," she said.

"I can't," he said. "Nobody can."

"Then fill me with new things to remember," she said.

"That I can do," he said and she brought one round, high breast to his mouth. He pressed forward and took in its sweet softness. Her long sigh was pleasure and there was something more, a kind of welcoming in it. She stretched her soft thighs out, letting her legs embrace him as she rubbed her Venus against him, already swollen with wanting. She pulled back, pressed her breasts into his mouth again, then drew away, her hand finding his hard rod as she gasped in delight. He felt her clasp him, caressing his throbbing maleness as little moans of delight escaped from her lips. She twisted her curvaceous torso, her hand pulling on him, urging, offering, and as he touched her dark moist place, Jody half screamed, half laughed, her fists pounding against his back.

"Yes, yes, yes," she said and came forward with him, surging with him, twisting and turning her pelvis to let every tiny part of her feel, touch, and enjoy. Where before she had been tentative, now she was eager. Where before she had only wanted, now she demanded. Where she had come in discovery and delight, she now came in the total pleasures of the flesh. Every part of her rubbed against him as she pursued ecstasy, yet somehow, the shy sweetness of her remained through her newfound wantonness. Small sighs came from her as he moved with slow, sensual strokes inside her, rising in pitch and intensity as she hurried ecstasy, becoming gasped screams and finally, a full-throated cry of triumph.

"Now, now, coming now, coming!" she cried as she wanted him to know what his flesh already knew. Her round breasts jiggled against his face, her convex little belly pushed against his abdomen. Entwined with him, her back arching under him as her screams rose into the willow trees, she clung to the moment, seizing rapture as if it were her own discovery, her own gift to give and to receive. When her cries spiraled to an end, her body remained against him, until she finally fell back onto the soft fern moss. He lay almost completely over her, nibbling and tasting the sweetness of her, and she sighed contentedly as he watched the little smile that touched her lips. Her soft brown eyes were looking up at him with warm sweetness and he was admiring their beauty when he saw her eyes grow wide, not in caring but in horror.

Her lips parted and as he frowned at her, the scream bursting from her as she stared past his shoulder. He started to turn when pain shot through his back, then his shoulder, and Jody's scream was drowned out by another. He fell from her and turned, the pain racing through him, and he stared at the tall form that rose over him, the long pole raised, the hooked point ready to plunge downward again. Transfixed, he saw a near-naked shape caked in red, breasts streaked with scarlet, long legs torn and slashed, hair matted with blood—a creature out of hell, a gorgon, a succubus risen from the dead.

He heard her voice scream and yet it was as if the sounds came from somewhere else. "You, all of it you, all of it you," she repeated, her body shaking off drops of water mixed with scarlet. "But I win. I live. And you die," she said. Fargo saw her arm muscles tighten as she drove the pole at him again. The pain in his back made him cry out as he twisted his body and the pointed hook grazed his ribs as it plunged into the moss. She was pulling it out of the ground to strike again when he saw the small, naked form flash past him and slam into Darlene at the knees.

Darlene fell sideways, still clutching the pole as Fargo saw Jody roll away. Darlene turned on her, raised the pole, and lunged at her. Jody gave way, backing up as the hell-creature lunged again. Jody's back was almost at the water, Fargo saw, her right foot slipping in the soft mud of the riverbank. He groaned and the pain shot through him as he reached out to grasp the Colt in the holster that lay on the moss. He managed to pull the gun out, and turned to try and steady it long enough to fire as his arm trembled from the pain that coursed through him. But before he could aim, he saw Darlene fling herself forward with the pole to plunge it through Jody's naked body. He cursed and cried out but saw Jody drop down to the edge of the bank on all fours. Darlene's berserk form slammed into her, pitched forward, and tried to twist her body around as she fell in a kind of grotesque somersault.

The strangled cry rose into the air, a rattling

sound, and Fargo looked on as Darlene's bloodied, slashed form rose, the pole deep through her abdomen where she had somersaulted onto it. With a last, gargled sound, she pitched forward into the river, thrashing her body one last time. Fargo stared as her body floated away with the pole rising from the center of her chest, and thought that it could have been a headstone from hell. He fell back, pain racking him, and Jody was soon there, kneeling beside him.

"It's over now," he said. "Evil doesn't die easily. Somehow, she was thrown clear when the logs came down. She was swept downriver, and probably lay lodged nearby and saw us when we bedded down here." He winced as another shudder of pain shot through him. She knelt at his side and looked at the wounds in his back. "I've some real good salve in my saddlebag and an old shirt you can tear into bandages," he told her.

She went to the Ovaro, returned with the salve in its horn bottle, applied it gently, and bandaged him with strips from his shirt. "This is going to need healing and stitching," she said. "There's a doctor in Hightop. Think you can ride that far?"

"No." He grimaced as another surge of pain overcame him. "But there is another place I might make it to. Then you can fetch the doc."

She nodded, pulled on some clothes, and then helped him partly dress and pull himself onto the Ovaro. She followed his directions as he kept the Ovaro at a walk. A strong moon afforded light. He found the pyramid of three stone slabs and then the forest of blue spruce and lodgepole pine. Dawn rose as they reached an area that had been partly cleared and the wood, canvas, and tar paper shacks came into sight. Figures came toward them and, through the pain and weakness pushing at him, he saw Jeremiah's towering form, then Jesse's full, deep-breasted figure, her sultriness reaching out as it had at his first visit.

"Help me," he heard Jody say, and then other hands were lifting him from the horse, laying him on a cot in what he recognized as Jesse's little shack. "He needs a doctor. Can anyone show me the way to Hightop?" Jody asked.

"I can," a thin man with a scraggly beard said. There was more talk but Fargo only heard bits and pieces of it as waves of faintness overcame him. He didn't know how long it all took as he passed in and out of consciousness, but when he awoke he felt the proper bandages around his torso, the pain now only a dull ache. Someone moved beside him and he saw Jody, then Jesse swam into view. "How long have I been out of it?" he asked.

"A few days," Jody said. "We've been taking turns changing bandages and putting on the ointment the doc gave us."

"I'm thinking I'm real lucky," Fargo said. "And grateful."

"She's the one did the most," Jesse said and nodded to Jody.

"Everyone here has been helping," Jody replied. Jesse rose and strolled from the shack. "Jesse told me how you came to know them," Jody said. "And how you stopped them from playing highwayman.

I feel sorry for them, all of them. They're all victims of things they couldn't control."

"A lot of them are victims of Tillman's legacy," Fargo said. "The doc say how long I had to stay here?"

"You can go soon as you feel up to it," Jody said. He nodded, and sank back on the cot, knowing that moment wasn't there yet. Jody slept on the cot with him, and his strength returned by the week's end. When he was ready to leave, he gathered everyone together, Jeremiah, Jesse, and all the other adults in the forefront of a circle, the youngsters listening behind them.

"I'll be coming back in a few days with some papers I want you to sign. They're called claim forms. I'll be paying the fees for each form. Take them to the land agent and register them. When I'm finished, this forest will be yours, all of you together. You can work it, do your own logging or charge others to log on it. Whatever you decide to do with it, the land will be yours," Fargo said.

"But it's Tillman land, most of it," Jeremiah said.

"Not anymore."

"He's got a daughter, Darlene," someone else said.

"Not anymore," Fargo said. "I'll be back. You just sign."

"I'll get the horses," Jody said and hurried off. Jesse came to stand before him, her sensuous, sultry visage tinged with a wry smile.

"Last time you couldn't stay because you'd promises to keep. This time you've your own woman with you," she said. "But I know how to wait. Maybe there'll be another time."

"Maybe," he said as Jesse's full lips touched his. She turned and hurried away before Jody brought the horses.

"I'm glad you're doing this," Jody said as they rode off. "It's like finding good where there wasn't any before." A sly little smile edged her lips. "Almost as good as discovering pleasures you never knew about," she said.

"Almost," he agreed.

"By the way, there's a hotel in Hightop. I reserved a room there when I fetched the doc . . . just in case," she said. "I'm not finished discovering," she added, leaning over and finding his lips with hers.

"You should never finish discovering," he said, and put the Ovaro into a trot.

LOOKING FORWARD!
The following is the opening
section from the next novel in the exciting
Trailsman series from Signet:

THE TRAILSMAN #210
THE BUSH LEAGUE

Kansas City, Missouri, 1861,
where progress was creeping into the West,
along with men who were trying to
use it for their own gain. . . .

"So?"

"They want to go to San Francisco."

Again, Fargo said, "So?"

"They need someone to take them."

"I told you," Fargo said. "I'm not interested in—
what's it called? Baseball?"

"Right, baseball," Meeker said.

Meeker ran the livery, the stage line and, Fargo
thought, had something to do with the railroad.
Fargo could only guess he liked the man because he
was a hard worker.

"Fargo," Meeker said, "they came this far by rail,
but they want to see the West. They want to go
cross-country to San Francisco, and they're willing
to pay someone to guide them there."

Now Fargo's interested was piqued.

"Do they have the money?"

"They'll pay very well."

"And where will they get this money they're going to use to pay very well?"

"They're gonna play baseball," Meeker said. "From town to town, city to city, they'll put on a game and charge people to come and see it."

"And people will pay for that?"

"They're payin' for it in the East," Meeker said, "and they paid for it here in Kansas City."

"When was that?" Fargo asked. "I didn't see it."

"They did it the day before you got here. You just missed it."

"Too bad."

"Are you interested?"

Fargo hesitated a moment, then said, "I'll listen to an offer from whoever's in charge."

"Fine," Meeker said. "His name's Arnold, Jack Arnold. He's over at the Silver Spur." The Spur was one of the finer hotels in town.

"He can afford to stay there?"

"He can," Meeker said, "but the other players can't. They've made different arrangements."

"Okay. And what arrangements have you made with Jack Arnold?"

Meeker looked . . . well, meek.

"I told him you'd come to the hotel to talk to him," he said.

"And what are you getting out of this, Ben?"

Meeker looked away and said, "A small finder's fee—if you take the job."

"Well," Fargo said, after a moment, "I guess there's no harm in listening, and I have been here four days already. It's time for a change."

"Then I can tell him you'll see him?"

"Sure."

"Three o'clock this afternoon?" asked Meeker.

Fargo knew it was now only about one o'clock.

"You already set the time?"

"Well . . . I'm tryin' to be helpful."

And make some extra money, Fargo knew. He laughed and shook his head.

"All right, Ben," he said, "three o'clock."

"Great." Meeker stopped facing Fargo and turned to face the bar. He waved the bartender over. "Let me buy you a beer."

"Don't you have to go over to the hotel and set this up?"

"Nope."

"You don't have to confirm it?"

Meeker ducked his head and said, "It's confirmed."

"Sonofabitch," Fargo said, chuckling, "I ought to make you buy me two beers."

At three o'clock Fargo entered the lobby of the Silver Spur Hotel. He was staying several blocks away in the less expensive—but still clean and decent—Kansas House.

He went to the desk and asked for Jack Arnold.

"I believe Mr. Arnold is in the dining room, sir."

"What's he look like?"

"Oh," said the clerk, "I think you'll know his table when you see it, sir."

Fargo shrugged and walked to the dining room entrance. The clerk was right, there was one table with a lot of activity. It seemed as if Jack Arnold was holding court. He appeared to be the slightly corpulent gentleman wearing the three-piece gray suit and holding a huge cigar. There were four or five other men who were swirling around him obediently. Some of them had pads of paper and were writing furiously. Fargo correctly assumed that these were members of the press. There was one other man, looking tired and unhappy, who was seated at the table with Arnold, apparently trying to eat a meal.

Fargo walked to the table.

". . . telling you gentlemen it's going to sweep the nation. Abner Doubleday will ride this game right into the White House, mark my words."

One of the newsmen asked him a question but Arnold didn't hear him. He was looking at Fargo.

"You look like you're in fine shape, sir," Jack Arnold said as Fargo approached his table.

"Thanks," Fargo replied.

"Would you like to play ball?"

"Ball?"

"Baseball?"

"No," Fargo said, "I have no interest in baseball. Are you Jack Arnold?"

"I am, indeed, sir. What can I do for you?"

"We have a three o'clock appointment."

Arnold looked very pleased and hastily stood up, reaching for Fargo's hand, switching the cigar to his left.

"Skye Fargo, then?"

"That's right."

He allowed the Easterner to pump his hand enthusiastically for a while before reclaiming it. Arnold once again took hold of the cigar with his right hand.

"All right, gents, that's all for now," Arnold said. "We can talk again later."

"What kind of business do you have with the Trailsman, Mr. Arnold?" one of the men asked.

"Private business, son," Arnold said coldly. "Off with you."

The members of the press went off, buzzing amongst themselves about what a meeting with "Big" Jack Arnold and the Trailsman meant.

"Please, Mr. Fargo, have a seat."

Fargo sat.

"This is Mike Flowers, my manager."

"Manager?"

"He manages the baseball team," Arnold said, but Fargo still didn't know quite what that meant.

"Glad to meet you," he said, shaking hands with the man anyway. He then looked at Arnold. "I understand you want to travel overland to San Francisco."

"We do, indeed, sir, and with many stops inbetween. We want to see the country, and show it our wares."

Fargo refrained from asking, "What wares?" because he knew the man would just start talking about baseball again, leaving Fargo in a fog.

"I have been told that you're the man to take us on this journey."

"I am," Fargo said, "if the price is right."

Arnold sat back and puffed on his cigar. "I don't think you'll find the money a problem, sir," he said. Abruptly he looked at Flowers and said, "Mike, I'd like to conduct this business with Mr. Fargo alone, if you don't mind."

"I haven't finished eating," Flowers complained.

Arnold smiled patiently.

"There's an empty table right over there."

Flowers looked over at the table Arnold indicated, then picked up his plate and walked over to it. He sat down and resumed eating.

"The man has no social graces," Arnold said. "It's a wonder he can handle a baseball team as well as he can."

"Can he?"

"He's the best manager in the league."

Fargo had no idea what that meant, since he had no idea how many baseball teams there were. And he still wasn't sure he knew what a baseball manager was.

"Let's get down to business, Mr. Fargo," Arnold said. He took out a piece of paper and wrote down a number, then slid it over to Fargo, who looked at it. "That's for seeing us safely across country to San Francisco." He wrote another number on a different slip of paper. "That's a bonus when we get there, all in one piece. What do you think?"

Fargo looked at the two pieces of paper.

"Frankly, it's very generous, Mr. Arnold," he said. "Almost *too* generous. Are you expecting trouble?"

"With what we read about the West back East, Mr. Fargo, yes, I expect it."

"What you read is exaggerated."

"Yellow journalism?"

Fargo wasn't exactly sure what that meant but it sounded right. He didn't respond, though.

"Well, if only half of what we've read is correct, I think we'll still need a guide. That's what the figure on the first piece of paper is for. The figure on the second is for . . . well, let's call it being a 'bodyguard.' "

"Why the slips of paper?"

"I never discuss money out loud in public," Arnold answered. "I think it's bad luck—and you never know who's listening."

Fargo looked around, but no one seemed to be listening at that moment.

"What do you say, sir?" Arnold urged.

Fargo hesitated, then turned over one of the slips of paper Arnold had written on. He reached over, picked up the pencil Arnold had used, wrote the word *yes* on the paper, and passed it over to the man.